Nobody should have been there.

But Jacoba's startled gaze met that of a man who strode through the door as though on cue. Mind spinning, she ignored the feverish shiver that ran the length of her spine as her fingers tightened on the drape.

Tall, effortlessly elegant in the stark black and white of his evening clothes, the newcomer moved with a leashed, vital energy that hooked into something hidden and vulnerable in Jacoba. The breath caught in her throat as her gaze roamed a Mediterranean face honed into formidable angularity, olive skin a startling contrast to pale eyes—eyes that locked onto her.

Prince Marco Considine of Illyria walked towards her, his arrogant features taut and intent, as though she were the only person in the room.

In a purely instinctive gesture, one gloved fist covered her heart, protecting it from the overpowering impact of a man she'd avoided for the past ten years.

Royalty, revenge, seduction and intrigue in—

THE ROYAL HOUSE OF ILLYRIA

A EUROPEAN ROYAL DYNASTY

THE ROYAL HOUSE OF ILLYRIA, featuring
Prince Gabriele Considine, Grand Duke of Illyria, his
brother Prince Marco and their sister Princess Melissa.

AN INTERNATIONAL SCANDAL

Royal jewels, known as the Queen's Blood,
have been taken. Who stole them?
Was it really Gabriele's fiancée?

ROYAL PASSIONS UNLEASHED

For Gabriele, Marco and Melissa,
the search to uncover the truth gives way
to royal heartbreak, passion and desire!

THE PRINCE'S CONVENIENT BRIDE

BY
ROBYN DONALD

MILLS & BOON®

First published in Great Britain 2007
Harlequin Mills & Boon Limited,
Eton House, 18-24 Paradise Road, Richmond, Surrey TW9 1SR

© Robyn Donald 2007

ISBN-13: 978 0 263 19561 3
ISBN-10:   0 263 19561 9

Set in Times Roman 10½ on 12 pt
07-0107-51519

Printed and bound in Great Britain
by Antony Rowe Ltd, Chippenham, Wiltshire

THE PRINCE'S CONVENIENT BRIDE

CHAPTER ONE

IT WAS, Jacoba Sinclair decided, the perfect setting for an evening of high romance. A full moon sailed across the sky, burnishing the panorama of mountains with heartbreaking glamour and silhouetting their rounded, muscular shapes above a lake that shone with the glossy blackness of obsidian.

In stark contrast, the people inside the building drank champagne in the sort of clothes seen only at very formal balls. Light from the huge Venetian chandelier gleamed on bare shoulders adorned with jewels, their warm glow highlighting the seductive glimmer of satin and the elegant austerity of men's evening clothes. Candle flames bobbed from tables set with crystal and silver and festooned with white and gold flowers.

Jacoba smoothed a hand over her hip, her long fingers skimming the crimson silk that billowed out with subtle sensuality from a tiny waist into an extravagant skirt. The gems in her tiara caught fire from the chandelier, each diamond pulsing with cold, clear fire.

They were genuine, like the stones in the drop earrings and the necklace—and worth an obscene amount of money. The mountains and the lake, and the Southern Cross emblazoned across the clear New Zealand sky, were real too, their raw permanence mocking the transitory glitter of the room.

Because everything else inside was as fake as the furs that draped the wall behind her. By day the exotic pavilion led a workaday life as a restaurant at the top of a ski lift, and the elegantly dressed men and women sipping imitation champagne had been hired for their patrician faces and sleek bodies.

Like her.

This was her life. She was being paid a vast amount to smile, to look haughty and seductive, as expensive and unattainable as the gems that blazed at her throat and hung from her ears.

'Perfect,' Zoltan said throatily. 'Yes, like that, looking down at the lake, then turn—and see your prince. I want a kind of stunned wonder, followed by just the beginnings of a smile, all your glossy confidence transmuted into a flash of wistful longing.' He paused before adding snidely, 'Think you can do that?'

Jacoba knew he'd been lured to direct the advertisement by huge money and the promise of a prestigious campaign— and that he'd wanted a Hollywood screen goddess to play her part. Tired of being addressed as though she were a five-year-old, she decided to show him that models knew a thing or two about acting.

'I think I can manage that,' she drawled, her voice pitched low, and turned her head to fix him with the look he wanted.

Zoltan gave her a sharp glance. 'All right, let's see it for the camera,' he said curtly.

Ignoring his open scepticism she switched her attention to the magnificent view, pulling back an artificial taffeta curtain. She recalled how it had felt to look at other families when she'd been a kid, how she'd watched children play with their parents and wondered why she didn't have a father…

'Great,' the director said, not bothering to hide his surprise. 'OK, catch some movement on the other side of the room, look across, and see him. Slowly now…'

His voice rattled on, tearing at her concentration. Perhaps he'd heard that some photographers used a barrage of talk at fashion shoots to enthuse and inspire models. Irritated, Jacoba tuned him out.

The extras played their roles, chatting, flirting and laughing softly. Ignoring the camera, she let her gaze drift over the crowd, move on slowly towards the door at the back, find the one particular man who'd just walked in through the door...

Nobody should have been there. Sean Abbott, the actor who played her lover, was confined to the Lodge with a stomach bug. They'd decided to shoot around his absence, using a body double who'd dance with her.

But Jacoba's startled gaze met that of a man who strode through the door as though on cue. Mind spinning, she ignored the feverish shiver that ran the length of her spine as her fingers tightened on the curtain.

This wasn't the double!

Tall, effortlessly elegant in the stark black and white of his evening clothes, the newcomer moved with a leashed, vital energy that hooked into something hidden and vulnerable in Jacoba. The breath caught in her throat as her gaze roamed a Mediterranean face honed into formidable angularity, olive skin a startling contrast to pale eyes—eyes that locked on to her.

The noise faded until all she could hear was the rapid thunder of her heartbeat while Prince Marco Considine of Illyria walked towards her, his arrogant features taut and intent as though she were the only person in the room.

In a purely instinctive gesture, one gloved fist covered her heart, protecting it from the overpowering impact of a man she'd avoided for the past ten years.

'Brilliant,' the director said eagerly. 'Yeah, keep it like that—OK, cut!'

He turned, and his expression hardened. 'What the

hell—?' he began explosively, only to rein in his aggression when he recognised the man coming towards them. An ingratiating note appeared in his voice, 'Ah, Prince Marco—I didn't expect you.'

The comment ended in an upward inflection that conveyed a question he dared not ask; it wouldn't be prudent to quiz one of the most powerful men in the world about his actions.

Especially not when he controlled the huge cosmetics conglomerate that was spending millions on publicity for their first perfume, Jacoba thought cynically.

By then she'd composed her face into a mask—proud, aloof, almost disdainful. She stood very still, letting her breath ease out between tense lips, trying to minimise the space she took up.

Difficult for a woman with hair the colour of a tropical sunset who stood six feet in heels, wearing a dress designed specifically to catch every eye and enough jewels to outshine the southern sky! She fought back a panic-stricken giggle— a shock response left over from childhood—and concentrated on the conversation between the two men.

'I'm staying at the Lodge in Shipwreck Bay,' Prince Marco said, his voice cool and deep and English-accented. 'So I thought I'd come up and see how things were going.'

Jacoba's stomach knotted. She too was staying at the Lodge.

But she could deal with that. Like the rest of the world, he had absolutely no idea who she really was. Her parents— actors in the terrifying, unremembered drama that had been her infancy in Illyria—were now dead. And a lot had happened in the past few years in the small, impoverished princedom between the European heartland and the sunny Mediterranean. With the dreaded cadres of the Illyrian secret police disbanded, she and her sister Lexie were safe from them, and it didn't seem likely that in the twenty-first century her mother's other fear, the blood feud, would still be part of Illyrian life.

Anyway, the prince, born and brought up in his mother's country of France, wouldn't care.

She stole a glance at him, and a superstitious shudder iced her skin.

He'd care. Marco Considine looked as though he believed in revenge. Morbidly, Jacoba found herself recalling stories from Illyria's history—ancient tales of wars to avenge honour...

Don't be an idiot, she commanded, furious with her overactive imagination.

She switched her attention to the crowd, but there was no escaping the prince's overwhelming impact. Height had a lot to do with it; she'd probably never have done so well in the modelling world if she hadn't been so tall. And he topped her by at least four inches. Add his powerful build and lethal male grace, and he quite literally dominated the room.

But the strong framework of his face proclaimed an intangible, inherent authority. He was a Considine, boasting a heritage that reached back into the ages of myth.

Younger brother to the Grand Duke of Illyria—who was second in position only to the ruling prince—Marco Considine would have been raised with the same attachment to their castle in the mountains, the same pride in the history of their illustrious family.

And he was therefore dangerous, and forbidden.

Jacoba dragged in a sharp breath, and Prince Marco's gaze settled on her for a second before moving back to the director. Only a moment, yet she felt as though his steel-blue gaze had penetrated her innermost secrets.

Panic turned her witless, but she fought through it. He didn't know she was Illyrian by birth too. Apart from her sister, no one did—well, only her oldest and best friend, and Hawke would never tell. To everyone else she was a New Zealander. Her name, coupled with fair skin and brilliant hair, made most people assume she had Scottish connections.

She forced her mind away from the dark shadow of the past to wonder why the prince was wearing evening dress. The garments fitted him with the precision that indicated a superb tailor, subtly emphasising those broad shoulders and narrow hips, and his long, heavily muscled legs. He made every other man in the room look synthetic, a colourless imitation of the real thing.

OK, she told herself angrily, so he was gorgeous, a truly impressive hunk of a man. But she had worked with some of the most beautiful men in the world; goggling at him like a schoolgirl was embarrassing.

Composing her face into a serenity she was far from feeling, she forced her attention back to his conversation with Zoltan.

The prince said deliberately, 'I hope everything is going well.'

'Very well,' the director assured him, and embarked on a swift run-down of progress so far.

Jacoba was accustomed to being valued only for her decorative appeal, but this was the first time she'd been so comprehensively ignored.

Perhaps I'm getting spoiled, she thought wryly. Just as well I'd decided to give up this life.

She'd always intended to retire in three years' time when she reached thirty, but the astonishing payment for this campaign meant she could finish immediately—well, once she'd worked through the two bookings left…

In spite of the brevity of the conversation, she sensed in the prince a formidable, decisive intellect and an unyielding will that intrigued her. An interesting man, this scion of the house of Considine—and, she thought after a swift glance at his compelling, imperious face, a dangerous one.

As though he sensed her attention, his cold blue eyes met hers, clashing in a primitive, heady challenge.

She held his gaze for a couple of seconds, then let her lashes hide her thoughts, but she could feel his gaze as he said smoothly and with just a hint of censure in the deep, slightly abrasive voice, 'We haven't met.'

'Sorry,' the director said shortly, 'I didn't realise. This is Jacoba Sinclair.'

The omission of the rest of the introduction was deliberate, but it didn't sting. She had better things to do than obsess over stupid men who considered fashion models a lower form of life.

Summoning her most aloof smile for the prince, she held out her hand. 'How do you do, sir?' she said coolly.

'Ms Sinclair.' He lifted her hand almost to his lips, dropping a formal kiss into the air just above the glove.

In anyone else she'd have thought the gesture unbearably pretentious, but somehow the prince turned it into a sensuous invitation. A sliver of sensation knifed its way through her. She realised she was breathing more rapidly and she needed a large slug of that ersatz champagne to wet her suddenly dry mouth and throat.

Dangerous indeed! she thought, trying hard to be dismissive.

'My name is Marco Considine,' he said pleasantly as he straightened up, but his astonishing blue eyes were direct and uncompromising.

And appreciative. Jacoba had seen the glitter of lust too often not to recognise it, even though this man's formidable self-possession kept his features under control.

Her heart rate surged.

Beside her Zoltan moved uneasily. As well he might; he'd

just been reminded that Prince Marco held all the power in this situation. Oh, he'd have a contract, but Jacoba had no doubt that the prince would terminate it with characteristic ruthlessness if he wanted to.

Meanly, it amused her when the director rushed in with some innocuous comment about their luck with the weather.

Marco Considine's black brows drew together in a frown, but he turned his attention to the other man. Jacoba didn't dare allow herself to relax. She felt shocked and oddly exposed, as though she'd been pinned by a spotlight, held there by the force of the prince's will.

'So when will you finish?' he asked.

The director told him, 'We have to be out of here by six o'clock in the morning, but it will probably be in the can before then. Jacoba is taking direction remarkably well.'

Patronising jerk. Jacoba showed her perfect teeth and said drily, 'You're too kind.'

'So where is her partner?' the prince enquired in a neutral voice, although she'd bet her year's income that he'd filed the little exchange away. 'Isn't there supposed to be a passionate waltz?'

Zoltán spread his hand and shrugged. 'Sean Abbott is suffering from a bout of stomach flu.'

Black brows met above an arrogant blade of a nose. 'Is this a problem?'

'No,' the director said briskly, not looking at Jacoba. 'He'll be in all the close-ups, but for tonight we're using a stand-in and shooting around him.'

The prince nodded. 'Do you mind if I watch?'

Jacoba most emphatically did, but she knew better than to protest. Sure enough, Zoltán said heartily, 'Not at all!'

The prince looked at her, his eyes narrowed a little. 'No problem?'

Jacoba smiled. Just as heartily as the director, she said, 'No, sir.'

But there was. Marco watched the stand-in fumble another dance step, and wondered how any man could be so clumsy when his partner moved like a dream. Perhaps he was over-whelmed at the prospect of dancing with the famous—and outrageously beautiful—Jacoba Sinclair.

She was doing her best to cover for the man's inadequacy, but even her grace couldn't give him any sense of rhythm. Wondering if the colour of her hair—the exact fiery hue of her dress—was genuine, Marco glanced at his watch.

Zoltan shouted, 'Cut!' He moderated his voice. 'OK, no offence, but it's not going to work.'

The body double scowled petulantly. 'She won't follow.'

Marco said calmly, 'Will I do?'

The director stared at him, his astonishment obvious.

Sardonically amused, Marco continued, 'I'm roughly the same height and build, and if I can't dance well enough you can send me packing.'

He didn't look at Jacoba Sinclair, but he could sense her consternation. It was a reaction he wasn't used to; from his sixteenth year he'd never wanted a woman he couldn't have.

But she certainly wasn't sending out lures. Perhaps she was truly in love with the man whose mistress she'd been for some years, even though Hawke Kennedy wasn't faithful to her.

'Well,' the director said doubtfully, 'if you're sure…'

'You've nothing to lose,' Marco said with cool assurance. His offer had been a rare moment of impulse, but he wanted to know what Jacoba Sinclair felt like in his arms.

'OK, see how you go,' the director said, hiding his reluc-tance with an almost convincing smile. 'And remember, Jacoba, you're stunned and already half in love. I want emotion and that first excitement of plunging into waters that are way, way above your head. Show with your body that he only has to ask and you're his.'

Faint colour tinged her skin, and Marco smiled, something untamed and intense stirring to life deep inside him.

Leashing it, he listened intently as Zoltan gave his instructions, stating what he wanted to happen and where they should go.

It took longer than Marco expected to film their slow walk towards each other, the meeting in the middle of the dance floor. He found the process tedious, but it was interesting to see how such things were done.

And Jacoba Sinclair was a consummate professional.

Which was just as well, because Zoltan was a perfectionist, his attitude towards Jacoba Sinclair coming suspiciously close to being aggressive. In spite of that, she gave what Marco considered to be an excellent performance—in fact, he could almost believe that she'd been burnt by an instant passion for him.

In other words she was an excellent actress, he thought matter-of-factly. There was nothing personal in her sultry glances and half-smiles. Yet he sensed a hidden tension in her, and he didn't think it was caused by the director.

Marco wondered if Zoltan had tried to get her into bed and been rejected.

Surprised at the cold anger that thought aroused, he concentrated on what he was told to do. Easy for him, as the ever-present camera didn't intrude; its lens was kept on his back.

'OK, good, that'll do,' the director said. 'Now for the actual dance.' He gave Marco a man-to-man grin that made the prince feel like punching him on the nose. 'Much more enjoyable.'

Marco let his brows rise.

'Yes, well, this is what I want you to do…' Abashed, Zoltan suddenly became brusque, ending his explanation with the comment, 'And if you get lost, Jacoba will make sure you're in the right place.'

Marco held out his arm; Jacoba placed a hand on it, and walked fluidly beside him into the middle of the floor. And then at last she came into Marco's arms with a silken flutter, a faint, purely feminine perfume teasing his nostrils, her slender, lithe body pliant and yielding in his arms.

He fought down a surge of hunger so intense it almost unmanned him. The music began again, a waltz that hinted of Victorian ballrooms and demure young virgins scandalised by the close contact the dance allowed.

Her face blank, Jacoba avoided his gaze and stared over his shoulder. He didn't move until she gave him a puzzled glance, and when he smiled he saw a flash of fire in her smoky grey eyes.

'Relax,' he murmured. 'We're in love, remember?'

Colour flared in her exquisite ivory skin and her generous mouth compressed. Without giving her time to speak, he swung her into the dance. He'd been taught to waltz by his French mother, a severe taskmistress. Someone equally as proficient had taught Jacoba Sinclair; gracefully, she followed him, lifting her beautiful face to his with an expression that simulated the dazed, heady sensation of first love.

Except for her eyes, guarded and wary as those of a hunted animal.

After half a minute he said, 'Why did you insist on leading the guy?'

She sent him another glance, grey eyes challenging through the screen of thick black lashes. Marco's body tightened and the hunter within sprang into alertness; he damned near missed a step. No doubt mindful of the director's instructions, she summoned a smile that promised pure seduction—swift and startled and yearning, so radiant that for a dangerous moment he wished it was genuine and meant only for him.

Until he remembered that she was Hawke Kennedy's on-again, off-again lover. He didn't share, and he had no intention of stealing her from Kennedy, who was a friend of his brother Gabe's.

Yet his body, already aroused by her closeness, was aching with carnal hunger.

'Someone has to lead,' she said, an intriguingly husky note enlivening the crisp words.

'And he wasn't capable?'

Another flash of fire in her great, smouldering eyes revealed her reluctance to talk to him. 'He needs lessons in taking the man's part,' she said, then folded her lips together, the flush deepening along her sculptured cheekbones.

So she hadn't deliberately made that a *double entendre*. And although her accent had been overlaid by an English intonation, he said, 'You're a New Zealander.'

Something shadowed her eyes, but it disappeared before he could fathom it out. 'Born and bred,' she returned lightly.

'From this area?'

Her shoulder moved beneath his hand as she shrugged. 'No, I'm an effete northerner.'

Marco had already met instances of the friendly rivalry between the two islands that made up the small country. 'From Auckland?'

Her mouth curved as though she were letting him in on a wickedly exciting secret. He had to remind himself—and his far too co-operative body—that she was acting.

'Even further away,' she said cheerfully. 'The winterless north, where frosts are a rarity and the humidity is a killer.'

'I've never been there.'

Amusement glimmered in her eyes. They weren't pure grey; gold flecks glinted in the depths like precious metal in a matrix. Forcing himself to be objective, Marco still found himself marvelling at her beauty; he was surprised that Hawke found it impossible to be faithful to her, and wondered why she put up with the man's well-publicised affairs. She looked too confident, too aware of her own worth to play such a drearily resigned role.

If she belonged to him, he'd be faithful.

And where the hell had *that* come from? He was always faithful to his lovers until they parted.

He'd let her stunning face and the feel of her in his arms get to him; she probably stayed with Hawke because he was rich enough to pay again and again for his infidelities.

Perhaps something of his thoughts showed in his face because she glanced away and her reply was cool and guarded. 'It's a glorious part of New Zealand, but then I'm biased.'

'We're all prone to bias,' he said, his voice cynically amused.

Jacoba wondered what had summoned that dismissive irony in his tone; it was reflected in his translucent eyes, so piercing a blue that they seemed to cut right through the armour of self-possession she'd carefully constructed around her inner self.

He went on smoothly, 'Perhaps you could show your part of New Zealand to me one day.'

His words checked her smooth glide across the floor, but when he automatically tightened his grip she picked up the rhythm again without faltering, her face inscrutable.

'Perhaps,' she said evenly, and smiled again. 'One day.'

She seemed to be looking into his eyes, but her gaze was fixed on his brows, and when he bent his head she looked away again.

Adrenalin pumped through her in a flood of energy. Over one broad shoulder, she caught sight of the director, motioning the other dancers onto the floor. He was grinning, so presumably he was getting what he wanted.

Why had poor Sean come down with that wretched bug? He was perfectly safe, so much in love with his new wife that he couldn't see any other woman.

Whereas the prince was terrifyingly attractive, and her body seemed to have developed a mind of its own, aching with a curious, expectant longing. In fact, she realised with a small spasm of shock, she wasn't acting.

This acute physical response, this intense awareness, was real. She wanted Prince Marco Considine and her body was making sure she knew it.

The director began to make circles in the air, nodding and gesticulating.

'I think he wants us to pivot,' she said, looking up into Marco's face as though he were her only hope of salvation. 'Can you do that?'

Without answering he swept her closer against his lean muscular body and whirled her around, forcing her to lie against him, her thigh against his as the dancers opened out to give them room.

A shaft of wild sensation shot like velvet lightning from her breasts to the soft juncture between her legs. She shivered at the betrayal from within.

'Cold?' the prince murmured, holding her a little away so that he could look into her face.

Cold? He knew she wasn't cold—that she was on fire, burning with awareness, every nerve on tiptoe, every cell eager and alert, with that sensuous pleasure spreading through her like warm, smooth honey.

How could eyes the colour of ice gleam with fire? A gasp escaped her when he bent his head and kissed her forehead.

The momentary touch of his lips set bells ringing in a glorious, exciting peal, blocking out the sound of her mother's voice, urgent and afraid. *Never, never admit you're Illyrian.*

Don't even have anything to do with them. It is the only way you will stay safe. Promise me!

Dimly she knew that the cameraman was getting everything, but the intrusive, all-seeing lens barely registered. Flooded by pleasure, she closed her eyes—also not in the script—and rested her head a second on the prince's shoulder, finding some sort of obscure female comfort in his sheer size and strength.

'Bloody brilliant,' the director shouted robustly, breaking the spell. 'OK, keep going.'

And they did, until much later the ski lift delivered them down the snow-clad slopes. The promise of dawn glowed pale pink above the mountains to the east. Clad in practical trousers and a jacket, Jacoba yawned, exhausted yet still overstimulated by the man who stood beside her.

She'd crash soon, she knew; this feverish excitement would fade as soon as she reached the refuge of her room.

Until then she'd have to be professional and distant. It should be easy. It always had been before.

But the memory of her mother's warnings, her terrible fear that someone would one day discover their secrets, warned her not to drop her guard.

CHAPTER TWO

ALTHOUGH the shoot must have been boring for him, Marco Considine didn't seem at all tired. He stood beside her, somehow blocking out the rest of the crowd, who were mostly quiet now apart from the odd muttered comment.

Covertly examining him in the waning light of the moon, Jacoba noted that although the arrogant framework of his face seemed more pronounced, his raw animal vitality was still potent.

Someone gave a prodigious yawn and, like sheep, everyone else followed.

Except the prince. Shivering, Jacoba looked away, unseeing eyes skimming over the eternal contours of the mountains across the lake. The long night had imprinted Marco Considine intimately on her senses. She knew the way his body flexed when he guided her around the dance floor; she'd never forget his faint, masculine scent and her elemental reaction to it.

He was at once completely familiar and totally alien.

Whenever she was reminded of the advertising campaign, she thought with frightening bleakness, she'd remember just how strangely safe she'd felt in his arms—and how threatening that security was.

A short distance away, several buses and a car waited.

'This way,' Marco said, taking Jacoba's arm when she hesitated.

Jacoba tensed. 'The director—'

'There'll be another car for Zoltan,' Marco said calmly. He inclined his head towards the road, where a vehicle was approaching. 'There it is.'

Some implacable note in his voice warned her that further objections wouldn't be sensible, so she went obediently towards the first vehicle. She didn't care if he offended the director.

The Lodge driver opened a door, nodding to the prince. 'Morning, sir,' he said. 'Morning, Ms Sinclair. Everything go well?'

'I hope so,' the prince said, and slid into the rear seat beside Jacoba without touching her.

Be sensible—he's had enough of touching you, she thought crossly, trying to curb her racing pulses as the car set off towards the Lodge. Even if he felt this fierce, primal attraction, Marco Considine was far too sophisticated to make any move with a driver in front.

After what seemed a lifetime of fighting off men who saw her as beautiful prey, she should be grateful for his restraint. So although she was almost painfully conscious of the silent man beside her, she kept her mind blank and her eyes fixed on the road ahead until the Lodge appeared, sprawled elegantly beside the black waters of the lake.

Marco insisted on escorting her to her room, even inserting her key. 'I'm not *that* tired,' she protested, but it was oddly sweet to be cosseted.

He gave her a laconic smile and handed the key back to her. 'You are. There are shadows under those misty eyes, and slight hollows beneath your cheekbones.'

His tone was amused, yet she saw a glint beneath his lashes

that sent a shiver of agitated excitement through her. And even if she'd missed it, there was an air about him, a prowling, predatory sexuality that lifted every tiny hair on her skin.

Hastily, before she left it too long and fell into a silence she couldn't control, she said, 'I know Zoltan's already thanked you for stepping in, but I—and my toes—are truly grateful. It would have been a lot longer session if you hadn't offered your services.'

He shrugged. 'Somewhere in that lot of extras he'd have found someone who could dance. Which makes me wonder why the stand-in was hired, as he so manifestly can't.'

Because he was Zoltan's boyfriend. But in spite of the director's attitude, Jacoba wasn't going to make trouble for him. 'He's the right height—there aren't many men who'd qualify, and none in the extras.'

An inclination of the prince's dark head could have indicated agreement. Or not; Jacoba suspected that very little got past that cool, keen gaze.

He handed her the key. 'It's been an interesting night.'

Firmly squashing a wild impulse to ask him if he'd be at the Lodge when she woke, Jacoba gave him a sleepy smile and walked into her suite. Turning, she said, 'Thank you. Goodnight.'

His eyes narrowed. For a taut, reckless moment she thought he was going to kiss her; her heart raced in wild, delicious anticipation, until his expression hardened and he stepped back. 'Goodnight, Jacoba.'

Before she did something stupid and completely out of character—like putting out her hand to draw him into the room— she closed the door and leaned against it, her pulse thudding as though she'd barely escaped from some great danger.

She'd wondered if he felt the same dark enchantment that possessed her; now she knew he did, and the knowledge was dazzling, exhilarating—and scary as hell. For the first time in her life she wished she were less cautious. Every female instinct she possessed told her that he'd be a superb lover—and if instinct hadn't come to the party, she reminded herself waspishly, she'd heard enough about his prowess between the sheets.

And on the beach, and in the shower...

Years before, she'd been on a shoot with a girl suffering the aftermath of an affair with Prince Marco Considine. Poor thing, she'd been dumped—in the nicest possible manner—when she'd inadvertently let slip that she loved him. The prince, it seemed, had made it obvious right from the start that he didn't want the responsibility of being loved.

And as well as being commitment-phobic, he was Illyrian...

Yawning, Jacoba went through her nightly routine before sinking into bed. However, she had to banish frankly carnal thoughts from her wayward mind before she could relax enough to let sleep claim her. And her last thought was a vague, barely articulated question.

Surely, after all these years and the death of the dictator who'd ruled Illyria, her mother's warnings about danger from the country of their birth were no longer applicable to her and her sister...?

'How do you do it?'

Jacoba looked up from her fruit and muesli. Although well after midday, the Lodge had provided her with breakfast on the flagged terrace outside her room. 'What?'

Mere Tanipo gave a disparaging glance at the crumbs from her own slice of toast. 'Eat so much and stay so slim.'

'Genes and exercise,' Jacoba told her, admiring the way the landscape designer had managed to give each room a private terrace while still taking in the superb lake and mountain views.

Her companion sighed. 'And how do you manage to

look so good with no make-up, your hair dragged back into a pony-tail that only a kid should ever wear, and six hours sleep?'

'Sheer luck.' Jacoba's tone was light. She retied the belt of her white wrap around her slim waist. 'You should have a glass of skim milk to back up that toast; protein keeps you going. And some fruit will help too.'

Mere frowned before hastily relaxing her brow. 'You sound like my mum.'

'Listen to your mum,' Jacoba said cheerfully. 'It's amazing how much they know. My mother used to say, "Eat breakfast like a prince, lunch like a merchant and dinner like beggar." It works.'

The other girl looked past her shoulder, her eyes widening. 'Speaking of princes,' she said in a hushed voice, giving Jacoba a mischievous glance, 'yours has just walked into sight, striding across the lawn as though he owns the world and everything in it.'

The prickle of sensation between her shoulders had already warned Jacoba. 'He isn't *my* prince,' she said firmly, hoping the heat in her cheeks didn't translate into colour.

Her companion gave a snort of laughter. 'He'd like to be! That was very obvious last night.' She got to her feet and said, 'I have to pack. See you, Jacoba, and thanks for all the advice.'

'It was nothing,' Jacoba said uncomfortably.

'It was not,' Mere corrected. 'I feel a lot better—and so will Mum—about going overseas now you've suggested I contact your agent. Thanks so much.'

She left in a rush, leaving Jacoba trying to finish her muesli while her nerves strummed feverishly. When Prince Marco stopped beside the table, she let her eyes drift upwards.

Her first thought shocked her. What would he look like without the well-cut jeans and the Sea Island cotton shirt that matched his eyes exactly, its subtle check emphasised by a stripe three shades lighter than his olive skin?

Even as she thrust away the image of him naked, her mind supplied the answer.

He'd look magnificent—like a god, the sleek musculature she'd noticed through his clothes coiling beneath supple, gleaming skin...

'Good morning,' she said, thankful for the small courtesies that eased day-to-day communication. Her voice sounded prim, a little too carefully composed, but that was better than the helpless eagerness she was repressing.

'Jacoba.' He surveyed her face with a smile that hovered between irony and an experienced worldliness. 'May I join you?'

'Of course,' she said automatically.

Marco Considine lowered his powerful length into the opposite chair and regarded her with his unsettling blue eyes.

'I hope I didn't frighten your friend away,' he said drily.

'No, she has to catch a plane.' If they could stick to this sort of conversation she'd be fine.

'She was the one in the white gown—the *ingénue* as opposed to your sophisticate,' he said.

Horrified by an ugly twinge of jealousy because he'd remembered Mere, she said colourlessly, 'Yes.'

'When do you fly out?'

Where was this going? She suspected Marco Considine didn't go in for idle chit-chat.

After a second's hesitation, she said, 'This afternoon.' She glanced at the watch on her wrist. 'In three hours, actually.'

He leaned back in his chair. 'I'm going on to Tahiti for a week.'

'How nice,' she responded cautiously.

'Come with me.'

The straightforward proposition sliced her composure

into ribbons. It also hurt some hidden, vulnerable part of her; in his glance she saw nothing but cool speculation, as though she was something pretty he wanted and could afford, a *thing* to play with and then discard once the novelty wore off.

Outraged, she hid her seething emotions with a slight smile. 'You're very kind,' she said calmly, 'but no thanks.' She wasn't some glamorous, brainless sex toy willing to trade her body for a short passionate interlude.

He kept her pinned with that uncomfortably penetrating gaze. 'Are you in love with Hawke Kennedy?'

'You're being intrusive,' she said crisply, despising him for believing the gossip about her relationship with the man she thought of as her closest friend—the only other person in the world apart from her sister, Lexie, who knew their background.

Marco's eyes narrowed. 'Last night you responded to me. You didn't want to, but you did. That doesn't seem like a woman in love with another man.'

Backed into a corner, she attacked. 'This is harassment and we have laws against that in New Zealand.'

'Or is it getting too close to the truth? He owns this lodge.'

'So?' she flashed, losing her famous composure for a betraying second.

'So is he paying for you to stay here?'

'No.' She clawed back her poise and looked at him with disdain, letting her voice chill into Antarctic frigidity. 'Ultimately your corporation is paying. I find this whole conversation offensive.'

He should have been abashed, but apparently princes didn't do shame well because he merely looked cynically amused. 'I hadn't realised you were a prude.'

'Insulting me,' she shot back, 'isn't going to get you what I assume you want.'

'And what is that?' he asked silkily.

'A temporary lease on my body.' She infused her voice with hauteur.

One straight black brow lifted; he held her gaze in a challenge so cold and clear and unreadable that she felt its impact in her bones.

And then, without warning, he leaned forward and took her hand.

His touch seared through her like an electric shock. Lost in some dangerous enchantment, Jacoba stared at him while her body throbbed with an erotic charge that terrified her.

Marco lifted her hand to his mouth and kissed the palm, his lips lingering in a sensuous caress. Savage little shivers scudded down her spine and her mind spun off into some alternate universe where the only thing that mattered was the touch of Marco Considine's mouth against her skin.

She tried to force her fingers into a fist. A wry smile tucking in one corner of his mouth, he let his fingers rest over the betraying blue veins at her wrist.

'At least I'd be faithful,' he drawled.

Jacoba bit her lip. 'No,' she said too loudly, because some desperate part of her wanted to surrender so much she could barely get the word out through her reluctant lips.

'You're sure?'

'Absolutely,' she muttered, tugging her hand free.

This time he let it go, but not before she'd seen the glint of satisfaction in his eyes.

Eyes wide and startled, she watched him get up in one smooth, graceful movement. Her relief was short-lived; he leaned down and kissed her startled mouth. Jacoba froze, but her body, somehow sensitised by the hours spent in his arms the previous night, flamed with a swift, ruthless hunger that came out of nowhere.

Gasping, she tried to pull away, but Marco took advantage of her helpless response and deepened the kiss, taking possession of her. Gentle, yet powerfully persuasive, his mouth lingered as he tasted her with exquisite care.

The next moment she was on her feet and in Marco's arms, relishing their strength as they clamped around her. When he broke off the kiss and stared into her eyes, his own half-closed and intent and dark, she whispered something—his name?—but the word was crushed into nothingness by the renewed pressure of his mouth.

Dazed into a mindless whirl, Jacoba raised one hand to lie along his cheek; she thrilled to the tactile luxury of fine-grained skin. He lifted his head and kissed the corner of her lips, and then the lobe of her ear, and the spot where a pulse beat violently in her throat.

His hand cupped her breast. Pleasure thrummed through her in an incandescent tide, electrifying her. She'd always been so careful when it came to men, dropping her guard only with Hawke, who was almost a brother to her; never before had she felt this hot excitement, so exhilarating that she understood why people became addicted to it.

It's just sex, some part of her whispered. Nothing serious; just mindless animal attraction.

Her breasts ached with unfamiliar hunger, tight and receptive beneath his slow, infinitely knowledgeable caress. In the pit of her stomach something unfurled, a craving for more…

Then Marco kissed her as though she were the other half of him, as though they were going to part and never see each other again and this was to be all they'd ever have.

He ended it abruptly, setting her free and saying harshly, 'I must be mad!'

Bewildered and shocked, Jacoba dragged in a deep breath and pushed a shaking hand through her hair. He must have slipped off the ribbon that held it in a pony-tail, and she hadn't even noticed!

'Both of us,' she said raggedly.

'It's all right—no one can see.' He looked down at her, his eyes hard and unsparing. 'I'm sorry,' he said, his voice arctic and formal.

Horrified, she realised that she'd been so lost in his embrace that she couldn't have cared less if the world had been watching. Clutching the remains of her tattered dignity around her, she stepped back.

In a voice she tried to make light and mocking, she said, 'I hope you enjoy Tahiti, sir.'

He gave a brief, humourless smile that showed his even white teeth. 'And I hope you enjoy wherever you're going and whatever you're doing. But keep this in mind—now that I know you want me I don't plan to give up.'

Heart jumping in her breast, she said unevenly, 'I might be the first woman to say no to you, but I mean it.'

He didn't try to tell her she was wrong. Instead he said abruptly, 'You're scared. Why?'

'I'm not!' She glowered at him, and pushed a tress of hair back from her face. 'I don't go in for flings. *Sir.*'

Astonished, she heard him laugh, a genuine laugh with real amusement. 'Neither do I,' he told her with level effrontery. 'And if you think that hurling *sirs* at me like stones is going to keep me at a distance, you're mistaken.'

Recklessly she said, 'I despise men who think they have a right to any woman they fancy.'

'Tell me without any dissembling that you don't want me.'

Goaded into indiscretion, she blurted, 'What has that to do with anything? I don't go to bed with every man I want. I have some discrimination!'

'So do I,' he said calmly. 'You've made your point—you

want me, but you're not going to ruin whatever sick relationship you have with Hawke Kennedy for something genuine.'

'You know nothing about my relationship with Hawke,' she parried.

'I know he's not faithful to you, so there's no trust, no honesty in it.' He paused, and when she remained obstinately silent he went on, 'And I know there's never been the suggestion that you've been unfaithful to him. You seem content to wait for him to come back to you each time.'

Even as he said the words he wondered why he bothered. Women were two a penny in his life; he could have any he chose. Yet here he was pleading for the companionship of one who clearly didn't want anything to do with him.

All right, so she found him attractive—other women had wanted him and he'd ignored them. Hell, some had confessed to loving him, and he'd broken off with them before he'd hurt them any further. He'd never asked for anything more than companionship and the free exchange of sexual pleasure.

And he'd never poached.

Now this woman was looking at him with her amazing eyes, grey and impenetrable as mist, intent on denying the physical magnetism between them.

She said crisply, 'Please go now.'

Centuries of ancestors who'd taken what they wanted— and often paid dearly for their actions—rose within him. Marco knew perfectly well that she had a right to refuse him, that forceful seduction meant nothing, yet he had to stop himself from snatching her up and making love to her until she admitted that she felt the same potent, heady desire that was fuming his brain.

But reverting to the simple, uncompromising standards of the Considines who'd ruled for centuries at the Wolf's Lair wasn't possible in this modern world.

'Of course,' he said distantly, his brain working overtime. He looked down at her beautiful face, saw a glimmer of—what?—in the depths of her eyes, and again fought back the primitive instinct to take.

He touched her cheek, watching her eyes widen in confusion. There were other ways to get what he wanted—and he was a strategist.

Yet the moment his fingertips met her skin, tactics went flying; pure hunger drove him to kiss her once more.

Although Jacoba read his intention in his face, she was powerless to reject him. It would be the last time she kissed him and she wanted it so much.

So she yielded, her mouth soft and ripe under his, until he lifted his head and looked into her eyes, his own resolute and compelling.

'If you need me,' he said levelly, 'call me.'

'Good exit line,' she said, not trying to hide the mockery in her tone. 'You'll be easy to track down, no doubt.' *Impossible*, she meant, and he knew it.

'A call to any of my offices will get you through.'

He turned and walked away, the sun gleaming blue-black on his poised head, his big body lean and lithe and as graceful as a panther.

Thoroughly rattled, Jacoba sat down again, forbidding herself to watch him out of sight. Her mother had never let them do that; an ancient superstition from her family had said that to do so would mean that the person watched would never come back.

So cold common sense told her briskly to keep her eyes on him. She didn't want him back.

'Where were you when I needed you before?' she accused beneath her breath, but common sense didn't answer. She said aloud, 'Dereliction of duty, that's what it's called.'

She turned her head, but it was too late; the prince had already disappeared behind the side of the building. Frustration and an odd sort of desolation gripped her.

Ignoring her shaking hands, she poured herself a cup of coffee and tried to assemble her thoughts.

So she'd met one of the Considines. Her mouth trembled and she had to put the coffee-cup down in case she spilt the liquid.

'Arrogant bastard,' she said thickly.

Oh, yes. And tough, and ruthless, and high-handed and spoilt. And sexy as hell.

The only man who'd ever had such an effect on her.

But the caution her mother had ingrained in her meant she'd never see Marco Considine again. Oh, possibly at the launching of the ad campaign, but she was sure he'd have found someone else by then, and she'd be safe.

Leaving the full cup of coffee on the little table, she got to her feet and went inside.

Jacoba had agreed to 'do' the New Zealand Fashion Week for a fee that made her agent threaten to faint with horror.

'I owe them,' Jacoba said, grinning a little at the image of her tough mentor swooning. 'They gave me my first break.'

'Eleven years ago, and each year you go back and work for them for peanuts!' Bella's sigh rolled gustily down the phone. 'You're too loyal, that's your problem. Stupidly loyal.'

'So you keep telling me.'

'I'm right. I'm always right. You *are* going on holiday after Fashion Week, aren't you?'

'Yes. I'm going to spend a glorious week in a bach in the very north of New Zealand.'

'Bach? What's that?'

Jacoba grinned. 'It's a very small shack on the most beautiful beach in the world.'

Her agent sighed. 'So you're slumming it. And without any mobile-phone access! I just don't get you.'

But buying the run-down farm had been the right decision. Miles from anywhere, it was Jacoba's bolt-hole; when she'd worked through her bookings she'd build a new house and live here...

She lifted her eyes from the laptop screen and sighed luxuriously as she gazed at the curve of pinky-gold beach. She could have stayed at Hawke's house further south in the Bay of Islands, but she needed solitude.

However, right now she needed a swim. She'd been writing since four in the morning, and her brain had had enough.

She stood up, scanning the bay. A storm the previous week had stirred up kelp beds along the coast, and because she disliked swimming through the strands she'd stayed out of the sea. Now, however, the sun shone down onto serene blue water, with no dark clumps of drifting, clinging weed.

One of the nice things about her cute little word processor was that she could write wherever she wanted to. She'd spent the last couple of hours in a deckchair beneath one of the huge pohutukawas that lined the beach.

After saving more pages of what she hoped might turn out to be an adult novel, she took the computer back up the beach to the one-room bach. Whether the pages were any good she didn't know, but they were only the first draft, so she wasn't too worried about their quality yet. All she knew was that she'd had the story in the back of her mind for so long she felt that if she didn't get it down now it might turn stale.

And, as her two previous books—written for the adolescent market under another name—had garnered good reviews, she knew she could write.

Yawning, she got into a bikini. She'd swim along the bay, shower, have lunch and then sleep. Under the pohutukawa, she thought complacently, glad that she didn't have to share the beach with anyone else. Humming happily, she scooped up a huge rug and her towel.

But once she'd spread the rug out, it looked so inviting she sat down on it. A minute or so to bask in the sun would be delicious, she thought, not trying very hard to hold up eyelids that had suddenly got very heavy.

Somehow, she drifted straight into a dream of the man who'd tormented her unconscious moments since she'd let him walk away from her at the other end of the country.

He said her name, in slow, tender accents, and smiled, and held out his hand to her, and this time she had no fear of ancient feuds so she could go to him. But when she tried to walk towards him the air thickened, and she found herself receding further and further away.

In the end, when she sank to the ground because she could no longer fight against the invisible obstruction, he turned and said harshly, 'It's too late, Jacoba,' and vanished.

Tears clogging her lashes, she woke with a start.

'Oh, for heaven's sake!' she snapped, and sprang up, furious with herself as she ran down to the beach and into the water.

Diving into its brisk embrace wiped the last drugging vestiges of the dream from her brain. Doggedly she swam the length of the beach but, although it was late spring and the water was warm, she found herself shivering, and, mindful of the risks of swimming alone, she turned and headed for the shore.

At first she thought the sound of the helicopter was a boat's engines, and turned to scan the sea. Fishermen were rare on this isolated stretch of coast.

After a moment's survey of the empty sea, she realised that the sound was approaching far too quickly to be a boat. And by then the *throb, throb, throb* of the rotors proclaimed the origins of the noise.

She watched uneasily as the machine flew low and purposefully over the hills that sheltered the bay. It was too late to make a sprint for the bach. Although she'd overcome the modesty that had embarrassed her when she'd first started modelling, she'd never been able to achieve the casual acceptance of nudity that so many other models cultivated.

Her bikini was too scanty to be receiving strangers, she thought uneasily.

CHAPTER THREE

JACOBA stood upright in the water, watching as the chopper turned and aimed itself at the beach. Hawke, she thought in something close to panic—it had to be Hawke. Had something happened to Lexie? Had their mother's fears of discovery and retribution finally been realised?

No. Common sense told her that Ilona Sinclair's fears were rooted in the past. The new ruler, Prince Alex, had set his country free, guiding his people onto the path of democracy and modernisation. Lexie and she were safe.

So who was this? She pushed the fiery flood of her hair back from her incredulous face, adrenalin pouring into her bloodstream as the chopper flew low over her to settle awkwardly on the sand. She half-ran, half-swam towards it, finally coming to a stop in thigh-deep water, eyes straining as the passenger door slid open and a man got out—tall and dark and lithe as he ducked and strode out of the way of the rotors.

Her heart constricted painfully. How many times since she'd left Shipwreck Bay Lodge had she seen a proudly poised black head in the distance and felt a rush of excited anticipation, only to be dashed to disappointment?

This time she recognised the prince instantly. Something in her bloomed, caught fire in incandescent radiance. She felt suddenly naked, but she had no place to go. Pride wouldn't allow her to sink beneath the water, so she'd have to meet him with most of her body bared to his cold, pale gaze.

The chopper's engines changed pitch; incredulously she watched it lift off the beach and head back towards civilisation.

Numbly, she stayed where she was, waves pulsing gently about her as she glared at Marco Considine, while her heart jolted into life again after long weeks of sulking.

He smiled at her, and her stomach dropped into free-fall. Until the helicopter had disappeared over the hills behind the beach, his eyes remained locked onto her face, examining her as though she were some rare specimen seen beneath a microscope.

Flushing and hot, painfully conscious that every nerve in her body quivered in a shattering mix of eager anticipation and apprehension, she waited silently.

'Hello, Jacoba,' he said smoothly once he could be heard.

'Why are you here?' To her fury the words came out husky and low, as though she'd been presented with a gift beyond price.

'I came for you, of course.' He forestalled her swift, unwise reply. 'We need more work on the campaign.'

Bewilderment laced her voice. 'Why?'

'The scenes at the lake are of no use.'

She frowned. 'All of them? Surely some can be used?'

'A few stills, possibly, but even with the cleverest editing the video is useless.'

'Is this payback time?' she asked with cool insolence.

His face hardened. 'I don't work that way, Jacoba.'

'And I don't photograph that badly,' she said, her skin heating at his contempt. 'But I wasn't accusing you. I know the director wanted an actress for the part—'

'It simply didn't work,' he interrupted. 'Not your fault, not the director's—I was the one who didn't fit in. It needs shooting again; there's a warehouse in Auckland ready to go. It took us long enough to find you.'

'How did you?'

His smile was a cool statement of power. 'Your agent, of course.'

Well, of course. No one—but *no* one—refused a man as powerful as Marco Considine. Not only had he set up his own very successful business, but when his cousin Alex, the Crown Prince of Illyria, had been called back to take over after the death of the dictator, the prince had handed his huge business concerns over to Marco. Who'd subsequently taken them into stratospheric success.

So Bella would have told him where she was.

'Why has the chopper gone?' she demanded.

One black brow lifted in irony. 'It's delivering another passenger to a lodge further up the coast, and will be back shortly. In case you're wondering, your very hard-nosed agent has already negotiated suitable extra compensation on your behalf.'

Acutely conscious of the large amount of glistening skin she was revealing, she straightened her shoulders. He, of course, was superbly dressed from his tailored trousers to a sleek shirt, its sleeves rolled up.

'Bella's a professional,' she said shortly, feeling completely unprofessional, 'and so am I. Of course I'll do what's necessary to make the campaign a success. It will only take me a few minutes to get ready.'

Marco lifted an eyebrow to devastating effect and drawled, 'I'll help you pack.'

A few minutes previously she'd been yearning for him—now that he was here she wanted nothing more than to get away from him. He was too dangerous; her foolish heart was already playing love songs, and if she wasn't careful she'd make an idiot of herself. Feet dragging, head held so high her shoulders suffered, she started towards him.

And then something long and slimy and tough wrapped around her calf, clinging to her skin. Yelping in shock and disgust, she remembered too late the floating packs of seaweed.

'What the hell—?' Marco's voice, hard and sharp.

'It's all right,' she said, but too late.

Uncaring of shoes and trousers, he was beside her in a couple of long strides. Grabbing her, he hauled her out of the water, demanding curtly, 'What is it? What did you tread on?'

'Kelp,' she muttered, feeling utterly idiotic but unable to stop her babbling. 'I can walk, it was just a strand…'

But he carried her onto the beach and set her down, holding her for a few moments until he was convinced she could stand. Then, to her astonishment, he dropped to his knees and ran a hand across her thigh, clearly checking for signs of a bite or a sting.

Heat bloomed in the pit of her stomach, a forbidden fire. 'I'm all right,' she said in a voice she didn't recognise—thin and faraway and drowning in desire.

A gull called, a low, crooning mew that echoed oddly in her ears. Jacoba had the strangest feeling that the earth had stopped in its track around the sun; her breath locked in her lungs, and she looked down at Marco's black head, at his hand on her skin. Suspended in sunlight and exhilaration, she couldn't speak.

He looked up, and read what she could no longer hide. One swift, lithe movement brought him to his feet. He smiled, and she read his intentions—and her body surrendered in a cascade of sensation that wiped out every thought but the hunger building like wildfire inside her.

Panicking, she put both hands on his shoulders and pushed, but she might as well have been trying to shift a mountain. He was rock-solid, the muscles beneath her hands firm but unmoving.

'It's all right,' he said, his voice hard and sure and totally, infuriatingly confident.

And then he bent his head and kissed her, and just as before, every sensible resolution was drowned in a rush of reckless need. Jacoba kissed him back, her mouth moulding to his as though it had been craving his touch.

His arms tightened, settling her against his aroused body. Transfixed by a thousand arrows of pleasure, she shivered, her lips opening as the pressure on them increased.

Somewhere in the back of her brain a few hazy warnings jostled for attention, but she ignored them, lost in an erotic craving that time had only intensified.

Marco's kiss, his closeness, fed that hunger with ruthless efficiency. It burned inside her, a passion that had been smouldering over the long days and nights, stoked by a series of erotic dreams and the sharp, disturbing memories of dancing in his arms.

Her feverish response undermined what little was left of her will-power. A moan caught in her throat when his lean hand found the soft mound of her breast, his long fingers cupping it with exquisite precision. The caress melted her bones in a swift surge of pure sexual need that drove through her and swept away everything but the passionate instinct to surrender.

And it felt so perfect—as though this moment, this sensation, had been foreordained; as though something had slotted into place in her life and she was never going to be the same again. As though at last she had found her true home…

Her bikini was too tight, its friction unbearable against her wildly sensitive breasts and the aching heat at the pit of her stomach. Shifting from one leg to the other, she shuddered when Marco slid his hand beneath the fine catch at the bra top.

'You don't need this pretty thing,' he said unevenly, and removed it in one deft, experienced movement, leaving her half-naked to his scrutiny.

A reckless excitement shot through her. Marco's eyes narrowed and their colour intensified into diamond heat as he examined her breasts, creamy against his tanned hand. She'd never felt anything like this desperate arousal before; more than anything she wanted his mouth on the hard little points that tormented her with their responsiveness.

She gasped when he picked her up and carried her across to the rug under the pohutukawa, but wariness had been over-whelmed by the tide of passion. The muscles in his arms and shoulders bulged as he lowered them both to the ground, ending up with her sprawled across his lap.

Hot-skinned, she hid her face against his throat and undid his shirt, her fingers fumbling as she wrestled with each button, her whole being so responsive she was aflame with hunger.

She ran her hands across the broad, sleek shoulders and chest she'd exposed. Her breath stopped in her throat. He was magnificent, sleekly sexual, his body honed to strength and power, his face angular and arrogant when he looked down at her.

Their gazes clashed in fierce need. He said on a harsh indrawn breath, 'You are so beautiful you make me ache.'

His words, his tone, melted the last tiny spark of resistance. Jacoba turned her head and kissed the swell of his shoulder, her lips lingering and provocative. His chest lifted and she felt the rapid upswing of his heartbeats, a heavy tattoo in her ear. Delighted by his involuntary response, she licked the sleek, fine-grained skin with delicate greed. His subtle smoky taste transfixed her, so entirely male—a physical expression of his faint, subliminal scent.

'Too beautiful,' he said as though it were a fault.

'So are you,' she told him, her voice drowsy with passion.

He laughed, a sexy, uninhibited sound that brought her head up.

'Save that term for the pretty men like Sean Abbott and the stand-in at the shoot,' he said, and bent his head before she could formulate an answer.

The kiss was almost brutal, yet she matched it, exploring his mouth in a primeval challenge, at once defiant and yielding. Sheer, wicked excitement licked through her—headstrong, intoxicating and terrifying.

His mouth on her breast summoned shudders of pleasure; she held her breath while he kissed his way to the centre, and shivered at the violent drumming of her pulses when at last he took the tip into his mouth.

A broken, inarticulate sound forced its way between her lips. Tense and waiting, she felt something vital inside her snap, its fragments drowned in the honeyed sweep of passion.

While his mouth worked its heady magic, he loosened the tie of her bikini bottom and slid a hand beneath the material to stroke across her flat stomach.

'*Si belle,*' he muttered, his voice thick and ragged against the silken skin of her breasts. In the same language he said, 'You make me drunk with delight…'

Jacoba spoke French, but she'd have known what he meant even if she hadn't. Although his tone was rigidly restrained he couldn't control the glitter in his pale eyes, or the flush of heat along his wide, Mediterranean cheekbones.

Matching his language, she whispered, 'It is entirely mutual.'

He lifted his head, his eyes suddenly speculative and intent. 'So how does a girl from New Zealand speak such good Parisian French?'

How could he shut off this passionate craving so abruptly? Chilled, she said, 'My babysitter was French. I grew up speaking it.'

Marco nodded, but she realised that he was storing this information somewhere in his cool, clever brain. 'Later—much later,' he murmured against her skin, 'you must tell me a little more about your upbringing.'

The drugging fumes of desire were fading enough for her to realise what the inevitable result of this would be. She lifted her head away from his chest, but before she had time to gather her wits, he kissed her again, and his long fingers found the source of all her frustration and pleasure.

With delicate, unbearable skill, he stroked in slow, deliciously frustrating torment. A burning heat rose from deep in her pelvis, racing like wildfire through every cell in her body.

Once more his mouth closed over the tip of her breast.

Then he lifted his head. He said in a hard, thick voice, 'You've been driving me insane ever since I saw you. Tell me now that Hawke Kennedy is your lover, and I might be able to stop.'

Shattered, Jacoba said, 'I don't—he isn't—'

He waited until she stuttered into silence, then said with ruthless persistence, 'Why do you stay with him when he so obviously doesn't love you enough to be faithful?'

Jacoba felt her face freeze. 'I don't have to answer that,' she said disdainfully, and scrambled to her feet, looking desperately around for her bikini top.

He rose too. He was angry, she realised with an inner quiver as she recognised the cold fury burning beneath his armour of self-control.

'Because he's such a fantastic lover you'll forgive him anything?' he said brutally. 'Because he offers some sort of stability? Because he blackmails you into it?'

When she gasped and turned away, he took her arm and swung her around so that he could see her face. 'Is that it?' he asked, the words gritty and forceful, his expression so aggressive she suddenly saw those ancestors who'd successfully steered their way through the violent, bloody politics of the Middle Ages and later.

'No!' she stated harshly. 'Of course he doesn't blackmail me! And we are *not* lovers.'

'Just good friends?' the prince mocked. 'I don't believe in that sort of relationship between two adults.'

Uttering each word through gritted teeth, she said, 'It happens, especially when those two were practically brought up as brother and sister. Now let me go!'

He did, but only to cage her in his arms. In spite of her anger, desire rioted through her in a potent, heady flood, clouding her brain. Jacoba drew in a jagged breath, meeting his piercing, ice-blue eyes with helpless intensity.

'Brother and sister?' he said, and smiled, a slow, sensuous movement of his lips that pushed her eager arousal up another notch.

She sucked in a breath and closed her eyes, shutting him out. Forcing her voice to keep to a level, toneless note, she told him, 'We grew up together; our mothers were single parents who had to work, so a neighbour cared for us, at first all day, later after school and during the holidays. People used to think we were brother and sister, and we've always felt that way towards each other.'

Silence spiralled between them, until he said in a low, formidable undertone, 'Look at me.'

Reluctantly, she lifted her lashes to meet his probing, crystalline gaze.

Marco asked, 'Why haven't you told anyone this? You must realise that everyone believes you to be lovers, and pities you for his supposed infidelity. Or do you get some sort of kick out of being seen as a modern version of patient Griselda?'

Her head came up. 'Who'd believe us? Anyway, it's no one's business but ours,' she said curtly.

'But you told me.'

Jacoba bit her lip. Yes, she had, and why? She and Hawke both valued their privacy and they'd found the whole situation amusing. And for her their supposed relationship had been a shield against the predatory males she met in her career. Most of the men who wanted to take her to bed were careful not to offend Hawke.

Uncannily, Marco echoed her thoughts. 'Why?'

And when she stared at him, her mind churning, he elaborated, 'Why tell me, Jacoba?'

'Because you made me angry,' she said curtly.

'Or because you wanted me to know that your relationship with him isn't one I need to be concerned about?'

'No!' Too late, she realised the trap she'd set for herself. She blurted, 'Didn't you say the chopper is due back any minute?'

She was right. Frustration set fire to Marco's temper. How the hell had he let this happen? He wanted her so much that he could taste the hunger in his mouth, feel it etch like hot acid through him. Somehow she managed to shatter the control he'd always possessed, even in sex.

Mentally he cursed himself for being so crass as to mention Kennedy. If he'd thought a moment, he'd have understood exactly what her reaction to his taunt would be.

At least he'd learned that much about her, he thought caustically. And it didn't help to have to admit that when she was in his arms he wasn't capable of thinking at all.

Her lips, made fuller and more passionate by his kisses, trembled. 'We have to stop,' she said unsteadily. 'I need to pack.'

Gritting his teeth, Marco fought back another violent surge of hunger. He saw the colour come and go in that translucent, satiny skin as she turned away and struggled to pull the wet bra top over her breasts.

He said, 'Here, take this,' and handed her the shirt she'd stripped from his shoulders.

Scarlet-faced, she shrugged into it, turning away to slip the shirt on and retie the knot on her skimpy bikini pants. He noted that her fingers were trembling and had to stoop to pick up the beach blanket to give himself a moment's respite from the urgent hunger that had him in its grip.

When he'd reimposed a fragile control on his body, he straightened up, unashamedly using his height and size to intimidate. She looked hastily away, as though the sight of him—lean and bronzed and icily aloof—scared her.

That sideways glance through her lashes made him wonder if she hadn't expected him to stop. Clearly she'd anticipated denunciation and anger. But then, she was a consummate actress. In the video she'd been a woman falling in love, her expression radiant and innocent and wondering.

'You're right. We'd better go,' he said in a level, judicial tone, and set off up the beach towards the shack.

The slight squaring of her shoulders and the adjusted tilt of her jaw revealed that she was clawing her confidence back, inch by painful inch.

Marco said with the silky distinctness that always sent his employees scuttling, 'Don't look so scared. I'm not an animal, to force a seduction.'

She didn't answer, but he saw the betraying quiver of a muscle beside her mouth.

'Not that it wouldn't have been hugely enjoyable,' he added. He waited until colour flooded her skin before finishing, 'For both of us.'

The flick of scorn in his voice tightened her nerves, but shored up her pride. It was useless to lie; he knew she'd enjoyed every one of the maddened seconds she'd spent in his arms.

Ignoring the heat in her cheeks, she said, 'Yes. I owe you that, I suppose.'

He lifted an arrogant brow. 'You don't owe me anything. And because we have to work together I'll make one thing plain: if there is a next time, it will only happen when you make it clear it's what you want.'

Her eyes widened, then her lashes came down. Deeply mortified, she said brusquely, 'Don't worry, you're quite safe.'

'It's a deal,' he said, and stopped just below the steps onto the veranda to hold out his hand.

When she hesitated, he smiled—a definite challenge.

Stung, Jacoba overcame her reluctance and shook hands with him. Electricity ran up her arm, re-igniting the flame she'd fought back only a few minutes previously. The glitter in his eyes told her he was feeling it too, that he'd initiated this contact deliberately.

Setting her jaw, she pulled away. 'If you want me to be ready by the time the helicopter comes back, I need to shower and pack.'

'It will wait,' he said indifferently, but he released her and strode beside her up the beach.

CHAPTER FOUR

MARCO followed her into the one room of the bach, looking around him with lifted brows.

He'd probably never seen anything so primitive before in his pampered life, Jacoba thought snidely. And, damn it, he took up most of the available room and all of the available air!

Aloud she said, 'If you wait outside, I'll get ready.'

'Will you be coming back here?'

'No,' she said abruptly, then wondered whether she should have revealed that much about her plans. But it wasn't worth making another long journey north again; in a few days she was due to spend time with Hawke at his house in the Bay of Islands and he wouldn't mind if she arrived a couple of days early.

He said, 'If you get me a box, I'll empty the fridge.'

Furious with him for being thoughtful, she snapped, 'Thank you. The chilly bin's over there.' She indicated the large insulated box that would keep the food fresh. But as she turned to collect a change of clothes, her eyes caught the wet hems of his trousers and his sodden shoes.

Mouth and throat dry, she said harshly, 'I don't have a dryer, I'm afraid.'

He gave her a satiric glance. 'Don't worry about it.'

When she dithered, he finished smoothly, 'Of course, I

could take off my trousers and drape them over the veranda railing. The sun's hot enough to dry them.'

Knowing that he was deliberately taunting her, she swallowed. 'If you want to, yes. I'll shower now.'

Why, oh, *why* had he taken it on himself to come? The tycoons she'd met previously had minions who did all their grunt work.

Probably because he thought he could talk her into bed, she thought, hot with shame. And he so nearly had...

'You have a shower here?'

'Of course,' she said crisply, grabbed an armful of clothes and disappeared into the bathroom, wishing fervently that she could take refuge in the shower until the chopper returned. However, the only water supply was an elderly corrugated-iron tank behind the house, replenished by rain from the roof. And in Northland spring rain had to last over summer.

Also, she had to pack. Racked with shameful frustration, she settled for her usual efficient and speedy scrub, then turned off the taps with a vicious twist of her wrist.

Once out and dry, she shrugged into cotton trousers and a floaty coverall in darkest green voile, skimming her hair back from her face before applying the merest shimmer of lip gloss. She wasn't going to hide behind a mask of cosmetics; it would make Prince Marco Considine too important.

Still fully clothed, he'd finished cleaning out the fridge when she walked back into the room; he gave her a long cool look before carrying the chilly bin through the door onto the veranda that overlooked the sea.

Even then, with her back to him and tossing her clothes into a suitcase, she felt his presence like...like a caress, she thought angrily, slamming the door of the wardrobe. Ruthlessly ignoring her taut nerves, she picked up her bags and took them out onto the veranda.

Big and lithe and totally relaxed, Marco was leaning against an upright and looking out across the bay. Although the gentle whisper of the waves would have covered the slight sounds of her progress across the wooden floor, he turned immediately, his handsome face a burnished bronze mask that stretched her already taut nerves as she deposited her pack by the rail.

'Give me that.' He straightened up and held out his hand for her laptop.

'It's not heavy,' she said, her fingers tightening on the handle.

He said with a cool interest that made her very wary, 'Is this stubbornness a characteristic of yours, or do you save it for me?'

With the aloof precision she'd been practising in the shower, she said, 'It's only a laptop.'

'I was brought up to believe that no woman should carry anything heavier than her handbag,' he said with an ironic smile. 'Or a child.'

A fierce, powerful yearning ached through her. Horrified, she realised she was imagining a child—*their* child—a little girl with her mother's red hair and grey eyes, and her father's proud features, softened by the promise of great beauty...

A low throbbing banished the fantasy. The chopper was coming in fast and low across the hills.

'Perfect timing,' Marco said with a cool, compelling smile that didn't reach his eyes, and took the laptop from her, hefting the heavy chilly bin in his other hand. 'Let's go.'

They reached Auckland in the late afternoon, landing on the roof of a building in the downtown area. Normally Jacoba would have enjoyed the flight over the city between its twin harbours, one opening out onto the wild west coast with long black beaches, the other island-dotted and benign. This time, however, she barely saw it.

Once in the air-conditioned confines of the building, she said, 'When do we start the shoot?'

'Tomorrow morning. You're staying in this hotel tonight,' Marco told her. He glanced at his watch. 'You have a meeting here with Zoltan in ten minutes.'

He'd withdrawn into a cool, businesslike attitude, setting up a barrier between them. Good, she thought savagely, fighting a sharp regret.

The large, airy suite looked east and north over the harbour. Although beautifully put together, it had the impersonal formality of a place decorated for guests rather than the owner.

She'd seen too many places like this, Jacoba thought, wishing herself back in the sanctuary of her shabby bach.

Not that it was a sanctuary any longer; somehow Marco had breached its walls. She'd never be able to go there without remembering him, she realised on an ache of despair. She glanced at the flowers in a vase, and asked, 'Why are you here?'

'To facilitate things,' he said abruptly. 'And—' The seductive chime of a telephone interrupted him.

'That will be Zoltan,' Marco said, picking up the receiver.

Jacoba gave him a dagger-sharp glare, which he acknowledged with a wry lift of his brows. 'Yes,' he said, and put the receiver down.

Haughtily, Jacoba ordered, 'Please don't answer my telephone again.'

The prince's smile held irony and understanding. 'Sorry, it was an automatic reaction.'

'You'd hate it if I did it at your house,' she said in a tone that came embarrassingly close to a snap.

Now why had she said that? She wasn't likely to ever be in his house. How did his mere presence fry her brain and loosen her tongue?

He examined her with hooded eyes. 'I'm sure you're far

too well-mannered to commit such a cardinal sin. The director's on his way.'

Although Jacoba wanted Marco to go, she couldn't order him out. As he held the power and the purse-strings he had every right to sit in on this discussion with Zoltan.

So she forced herself to appear calm and professional in the conversation with the director, while trying to ignore the prince. It didn't work; every time she felt his glance, her body reacted with uninhibited excitement, sending her breath swiftly through her lips and the quick clamour of her heart-beat drumming in her ears.

Half an hour later a somewhat smug Zoltan—surprisingly pleasant this time—had left, and she was sitting on the big sofa fighting an odd mixture of relief and chagrin.

'One day—two at the outside,' the director had promised.

'What time do we start?'

'Six in the morning—a car will collect you.' He'd glanced at the silent prince and transferred his gaze back to Jacoba with a sly smile. 'So go to bed early tonight.'

She had given him a glittering look. 'Of course.'

Clearly the man thought she was Marco's latest lover. He did, she admitted silently, have reason; although the prince hadn't touched her or made the slightest effort at intimacy, she recognised a subtle possessiveness in his attitude that exhilarated her as much as it worried her.

In spite of being convinced that she no longer had any logical reason to fear Illyrians, she didn't dare let herself get close to Marco Considine. OK, she might be pushing it a bit to worry about what the paparazzi would find out if they went looking, but the promise she'd made to her mother on her deathbed still held. She'd never reveal she was Illyrian.

So now she got to her feet and said to Marco, 'Thank you for taking the time and trouble to bring me back.'

He rose too. 'It was nothing,' he said negligently. 'I owed you—it was my decision to re-shoot the video.'

'I knew that.' She asked with a flash of recklessness she should have killed, 'What exactly did you dislike about the original takes? Were you too recognisable?'

His brows rose. 'No,' he said crisply. 'And how did you know I was the one who pulled the plug on them?'

'Because if Zoltan had hated them he'd have told me; he didn't want me, and he'd have been delighted with a chance to prove that I was wrong for the concept. So if *he* wasn't the sticking point, it has to be you.' She waited, and when he didn't immediately answer added, 'At the very least, you must have agreed with the person who made the decision.'

Marco found himself wishing that she was more like other models he'd met—so absorbed in her career that she had little time to give to anything else. This woman was intelligent, and when she looked at him with those huge grey eyes, so clear yet so unreadable, not only did she engage his body but also his mind.

Dangerous…

No, he refused to accept that. He didn't believe in *femmes fatales*—but he had to admit that she intrigued him more than any woman had since his callow youth.

'It had nothing to do with your performance; you're the consummate professional. There seemed to me to be a difference in atmosphere between the shots with Sean Abbott and the ones with me, and if I noticed it, others will too.'

The truth, but not the whole truth. He added, 'This is the first perfume the company has produced, and I want the campaign to be the best it can be.'

Again, the truth—but not entirely. She looked at him with those enigmatic eyes, her beautiful face aloof and patrician, a little tense but graceful with her hair falling like living fire down her back, and the raw power of hunger knotted his gut.

His voice hardening, he finished, 'A huge amount of money is riding on this.'

She dismissed that with a slight twist of her lush mouth. 'It always comes down to money in the end.'

'That's how the world works,' he said cynically.

Her swift glance accused him of hypocrisy. He added, 'You employ a very tough agent to see that you get the utmost money for your appearances.'

She shrugged and let it go. 'If you'll excuse me, I'll have an early dinner tonight. You heard your very expensive director give me his instructions.'

'Yes, and damned impertinent I thought it,' the prince said curtly.

She shrugged. 'He wasn't talking to you—it was directed at me. Directors are despots, but he's not likely to antagonise the man who pays him. As you say, money is how the world works.'

And because he didn't seem to realise that her composure was more fragile than tissue paper, she walked across to the door. 'Goodnight.' She forced a brisk, impersonal note into her voice.

'Sleep well,' he said indolently.

And then he was gone. Closing the door behind him with a ragged sigh, Jacoba leaned back against it, trying to coax her tense muscles to relax. None of her usual methods worked; her whole body felt strung on wires, still alert and jittery with frustrated desire.

At least she believed him when he said he'd leave her alone. She couldn't see Prince Marco Considine either losing his head to lust, or forcing a woman. That controlled pride was backed by an uncompromising strength of will. A man who'd accomplished as much as he had before he was thirty had to possess both self-discipline and a driving determination that made her shiver.

Ice and steel right through, to match those Considine eyes and that formidable, handsome face.

To him a woman would be a diversion, a pleasant way to relax—but he'd make love with the power and grace of his inherent sexuality...

She peeled off her clothes and turned the shower on to cold to douse the effects of her thoughts, but she couldn't dampen down the stark hunger that still burned inside her.

How was she going to banish those wild minutes on the beach from her mind—and her heart?

Especially as she was going to be seeing more of him. A series of parties around the world had been planned to launch the perfume, beginning with a gala ball in London. She was to partner the prince at every one.

She forced herself to eat some of the dinner delivered to her, and then took out her mobile phone. Punching in a number, she waited until her sister answered. 'Hi, Lexie. How's things?'

'Fine,' Lexie said cheerfully. 'How's your novel going?'

'Not.' Jacoba explained what had happened.

'Bummer,' Lexie said succinctly, adding with some indignation, 'And I don't believe for a second that your work wasn't good enough. That director's out to get you.'

Jacoba gave a wry smile. 'Don't worry about the director. I've dealt with worse than him. How's Australia?'

'Terrific!' Lexie, a vet on a working holiday there, bubbled with enthusiasm for some time.

When she wound down Jacoba said, 'Obviously you've added enormously to your portfolio of animals! How's your money holding out?'

'Fine. Don't worry about me—I'm independent now, thanks to you.'

Jacoba had begun to model at sixteen, a couple of years after their mother had manifested the first signs of the illness that eventually killed her. Although Jacoba had enjoyed the glamour of her work, her main ambition had been to give Ilona Sinclair the best medical aid. Too soon, when it became obvious that nothing would help her mother, she began studying investment strategy, determined that Ilona wouldn't die worrying about her children's future.

She thought now that if her career had meant nothing else, it had given her mother peace of mind at the end and provided Lexie with the means to follow a vocation she adored.

Her sister asked now, 'Is everything OK, Jake?'

'Fine.' But the word rang hollow.

'I can tell it's not.' She hesitated, then asked, 'Is that Illyrian prince still around?'

'Yes.'

Lexie was silent for several more moments. 'Do you think he's suspicious?'

'No!' Jacoba hesitated, then said rapidly, 'Sometimes I wonder if we're not being a bit obsessive about keeping our identities secret. I can understand Mama's fear, but things have changed so much now. Of course she was terrified of the dictator and his secret police. Now that the legitimate prince has taken over I doubt if she'd be worried. I don't plan to go around telling people I'm Illyrian, but I simply can't see that it would be a disaster if anyone found out.'

Lexie didn't answer the implied question. 'Mama might have seemed a bit paranoid about not ever telling anyone, but she had good reason.'

'Yes, but Paulo Considine's been dead for quite a few years now. I just think it's probably not so necessary to be cautious.'

'You've met the new ruling prince—Alex, isn't it? Does he look the sort of man who'd take revenge?' Lexie asked inconsequentially.

Jacoba hesitated, except that it wasn't Prince Alex's dark, good-looking features she saw in her mind. Instead, Marco's hard, handsome face stayed fixed there.

Revenge? No, but contempt...

Appalled, she realised she'd wanted Lexie to agree that they no longer needed to hide their Illyrian heritage. Although she'd done it unconsciously, she'd been trying to find an excuse to let down her guard with Marco.

'If you're thinking about Mama's tales of blood feuds, no,' she said swiftly. 'Prince Alex is a civilised man, not a murderous psychopath. Anyway, why should *we* worry about revenge? If anyone is, it should be the secret police wondering whether we're going to demand satisfaction for killing our father and hounding Mama out of Illyria.'

'There might be more to it than Mama told us,' Lexie said diffidently.

Shrugging, Jacoba said, 'There probably is, but it's past history now. Anyway, it's not important; I feel a complete New Zealander.'

'Me too,' Lexie said trenchantly. 'All that Illyrian stuff has got nothing to do with me. I just want to forget about it.'

A little startled by her sister's vehemence, Jacoba glanced at the clock on the bedside table, frowning when she saw the time. 'Fine. Let's wipe it from our minds. Look, I'd better go. I have an early call tomorrow.'

She went to bed, wooing sleep with a range of relaxation exercises that eventually won her the reward, but when the alarm shrilled the next morning she woke feeling exhausted.

'Busy night, darling?' the director enquired as she was being made up. The malicious intonation in his voice ruffled

Jacoba's nerves. He glanced at his watch. 'How long will it be before you're finished?'

'Jacoba, don't you dare talk!' the make-up expert commanded fretfully, glaring at him. 'It's going to take me another ten minutes to get the lipstick right, and after that we have to anchor that damned tiara into her hair.'

'Nothing damned about it,' the director said. 'It's worth about a million pounds.'

Jacoba said stringently, 'And it's heavy.'

'Shut up, Jacoba,' the make-up man shouted.

Ignoring him, Zoltan enquired on a sneer, 'So you're not aiming to be a princess?'

'No,' Jacoba said indifferently.

It was the start of a long day. Jacoba kept waiting for Marco to appear, and was both frustrated and relieved when he didn't. Filming with Sean was entirely different; she had to act with him, whereas with Marco she'd been helplessly reacting to his formidable male charm.

Professionally, she used the memory of how it had felt to feel Marco's strong arms around her, how her body had reacted with helpless sensuality, how she'd felt when he'd smiled at her...

It must have worked, because late in the afternoon Zoltan called a halt.

'That's it, girls and boys, fun's over.' His gaze rested on Jacoba for a second, then flicked past her. 'Or just about to start,' he added on a malicious note, 'for those of you who are going out.'

The tiny hairs across the back of her neck prickled. She didn't turn, but her skin tightened as she sensed someone's noiseless approach.

Still in the crimson ball-dress, she stripped off long satin gloves and put them down on a side-table.

Tall, the powerful lights picking out the tough framework of his unsmiling face, Marco stopped a few feet away. 'Finished?' he asked Zoltan.

'It's done,' Zoltan told him. 'I think you'll be pleased with this version. Jacoba and Sean struck sparks off each other.'

'I hope so,' Marco said with smooth indifference, his eyes so cold they sent a foreboding shiver down Jacoba's spine. Without looking at her, he said even more blandly, 'That, after all, is what they—and you—are being paid for.'

Zoltan said hastily, 'Of course. Well, if you'll excuse me, I'd better go and supervise a few things.' He smiled at Jacoba. 'Have fun.'

Jacoba summoned a cool smile while her eyes warned the prince off.

Amusement curved but didn't soften his beautiful mouth. 'How long will you be?'

Acutely aware that people around them were covertly listening, she told him, hoping that he'd take the hint and go, knowing that he wouldn't.

'I'll wait,' he said.

Furious and alarmed, Jacoba left the set. Fragments of her conversation with Lexie the previous night bobbed around in her mind. Had their mother any reason to be so insistent that they hide the secret of their birth? Or was it just a fancy fixed in a tired, pain-racked woman who'd once feared so much for the lives of herself and her two small children that she'd hidden with them on the other side of the world?

Whatever, Jacoba didn't want any further involvement with Marco Considine, prince of Illyria. It was too dangerous, and not just because he was Illyrian. He made her feel too much, turned her into a woman of sensual needs that shocked and dismayed her.

If he wasn't prepared to take her far from subtle hints, she'd just have to freeze him off.

Somewhere deep inside, an amused part of her wondered how she was going to do that. Whenever he touched her, she went into meltdown—and he knew it. Deliberately, she took her time about changing, hoping that when she emerged he'd be gone.

Yet when she came out of the makeshift dressing room in jeans and a white T-shirt, her hair scraped back from her face and with no more make-up than a brush of lip gloss, she wasn't surprised to see him waiting, talking once more to Zoltan. Chagrined by the wilful excitement churning her stomach, she felt the slow burn that signalled the birth of desire.

He looked up the second she appeared and said something to the director before striding across the floor with the forbidding determination of a conqueror, relentless and decisive, his pale eyes fixed on her face as though claiming a trophy of war.

A chill of apprehension cooled her. Because they were being watched, she allowed herself a reserved smile. Although he returned it, she sensed his unyielding determination, and the hand that caught her elbow gripped a moment before relaxing.

'How do you manage to look elegant in jeans and a T-shirt?' he asked, steering her towards the exit.

'It's standard uniform for models,' she returned ironically. 'Like the big bag.'

He examined it, swinging from her arm. 'What do you carry in it? The rest of your wardrobe?'

'Just about,' she admitted. By then they were outside in the cool, sea-scented ambience of Auckland's dusk. 'What do you want?' she asked baldly.

His straight black brows drew together. 'We're going out to dinner.'

The compelling intensity of his gaze made her heart

compress painfully in her chest. 'I don't think that would be a good idea,' she said carefully.

He didn't pretend not to know what she was talking about; instead his fingers tightened around her arm as they approached a rough patch of pavement. 'I want to apologise for my boorish behaviour yesterday.'

'We'll take it as given,' she said. 'Thank you. And I'm sorry too—I shouldn't have let it go so far.'

'Tell me about it over dinner,' he suggested, relaxing his grip.

'No.'

There, she'd said it. The word in all its ugly baldness hung in the air.

'I think you should,' he said calmly, but something in his voice tightened her skin apprehensively. 'So far you've been the consummate professional. Why start behaving like a prima donna now? It could rebound on you.'

'That sounded rather too much like a threat for me to be comfortable with it,' she said, fencing as openly as she could.

'Clearly you've forgotten, so I'll just refresh your mind. We're having dinner on a yacht,' he said smoothly, 'followed by a reception and a cruise on the harbour with a hundred other people.'

'I didn't agree to…' She stopped. 'This is business?'

'Of course.' He frowned. 'It was all last-minute, but you should have known. Did your agent not contact you?'

Jacoba bit her lip. 'She might have faxed through this morning,' she admitted. 'Or emailed. I didn't check anything before I left.' She should be running for the hills like a hunted doe; instead, she was trapped.

In spite of the prompting of her inner caution, a suspicious glow of excitement licked across her skin. The drab industrial estate suddenly seemed lit by colour and life, the heavy air perfumed by anticipation. Jacoba wasn't in the least surprised when they turned a corner and in front of them a rambling rose—so gnarled and old it probably no longer had a name—bloomed with scarlet explosions against an ugly fence of rusty corrugated iron. A car waited at the kerb, its driver sitting patiently inside.

'I can't go dressed like this,' she said.

'Of course not,' he told her, a note of irony in his voice. 'Clothes are waiting in the yacht.'

Judging them to be just outside hearing range of the car, Jacoba stopped and fixed him with a glare. It was a mistake; he was watching her with a quizzical amusement that attacked her resistance. 'How?' she demanded.

'The wardrobe people organised it—I believe you patronise a particular designer here who knows your measurements. She had a dress she knew would be suitable, and her staff found accessories. And I'm sure you've got cosmetics in that bag of yours.'

Although fanatical about skin care, Jacoba never wore make-up unless she was on show. However, she believed in being prepared for anything.

'Yes,' she said reluctantly, and let herself be ushered into the car.

As it eased away from the kerb, Marco told her, 'There's been plenty of interest in the video, and with a lot of the fashion-week crowd still here it was decided to capitalise on their presence to start the publicity ball rolling, if you'll excuse the cliché.'

It made sense…

The yacht was huge. Marco noticed her looking around with interest as they walked from the dock onto the deck. 'It's not mine,' he said. 'I prefer yachts with sails. This was built for a man who wanted comfort.' He paused, then added, 'Actually, it was built more for his wife and her friends than for him.'

A note in his voice startled her. She looked up at his profile, hard-edged against the lights of the hotel behind. Yes, it had been one of slight contempt.

An interesting man, Prince Marco Considine—raised in luxury, with the heritage of a long and illustrious array of princes in his bloodline, head of a huge enterprise, yet clearly he didn't think much of people who indulged in this sort of billionaire's showing off.

He caught her looking at him. His mouth hardened, and his eyes narrowed. A swift pulse of awareness made her stumble; his hand came out and caught her, and for a moment she was held against his lean, big body.

The violence of her reaction shocked her. Eyes widening endlessly, she stiffened her lax bones. His hands on her arms tightened a fraction.

'Your move,' he said.

CHAPTER FIVE

HER move? A reckless rush of hunger shocked Jacoba; if all it took to breach her defences was his casual touch, she was in real danger of losing her head.

But there was nothing casual in Marco's intent gaze, and although he held her loosely she sensed a territorial imperative working inside him. It wasn't personal, she rationalised feverishly; his ancestors had held their lands and riches with an iron grip and a slashing sword, and no doubt that instinct to possess was hereditary.

And he wouldn't take the initiative. He'd said he'd wait for her surrender, and the cool confidence that gleamed from his eyes told her he was sure he'd eventually get it.

It took every ounce of pride and will-power to say, 'Let me go, please.'

He released her immediately, but when he guided her into a huge, elaborately decorated saloon every sense sharpened into acute alertness. She felt as though he was herding her towards some unknown trap.

A servant appeared. Marco said, 'Please take Ms Sinclair to the stateroom that's been organised for her.'

The man nodded. 'This way, madam.'

On a silent sigh of relief, she followed the Steward into another over-decorated room.

'If there's anything you need,' he said, indicating a bell push, 'please call for the maid.'

'Thank you.'

Once he'd left she examined the clothes on the bed. No concessions to seafaring here! Her favourite designer had come up trumps with a serious dinner dress the exact colour of her hair. Long sleeves gave it an air of modesty belied by the deep V of its wrap-over front. High sandals, completely impractical and cut to display elegant ankles and narrow feet, picked up the glint of gold in the heavy crimson silk.

Someone had pinned a flamboyant fake rose to one side of the neckline. Jacoba smiled wryly, recalling the little rambler that had scented the air of the drab industrial estate. On the dressing table a flask of perfume persuaded her to sniff; it was subtly rose-scented with an undernote of exotic, sinful seduction.

No indication of a name or manufacturer—so this was almost certainly the reason for the campaign.

She sprayed it onto her wrists, waited a few seconds then held it to her nose. Rich and sensuous, it hinted at spices, but the aura of roses gave it a sumptuously romantic warmth that lingered in her consciousness as she put on her make-up, emphasising her eyes, downplaying her mouth. The occasion called for a looser, more relaxed hairstyle, so she left her hair down, grateful for its natural waves.

After dressing, she gave a moment's intent consideration to her reflection. The fire Marco had lit with his touch still smouldered, burning away her composure, but she'd have to resist it. Pride wouldn't let her give herself to Marco on the terms he'd laid down.

A knock at the door of the stateroom straightened her shoulders. Heart skipping a beat, she went across and opened the door.

Darkly distinguished and compelling in evening clothes, Marco stood outside with a security guard in close attendance.

'Bling,' he said succinctly, and when she hesitated, he added with an irony that didn't match the sudden glitter in his eyes, 'All the way from London.'

Her gaze skimmed across the famous name on the box he carried. 'Come in.'

Marco said, 'Wait here,' to the man beside him.

The security guard looked as though he'd like to protest, but one look at the prince's profile stopped whatever he'd been going to say. He stepped out into the hallway.

That effortless authority was probably just as useful to Marco as his brilliant brain and potent charm, other weapons in his powerful armoury.

'Earrings, I think, and possibly the bracelet,' he said, opening the casket. 'Or the ring.'

'Certainly not both,' she returned coolly. 'I hope there's no tiara.'

'Not on this occasion.'

'That ring looks as though it should only be worn to a coronation.'

'Think impact,' he advised, and startled her by slipping the huge, heart-shaped diamond onto her finger.

Without looking at him she picked up the earrings, obviously made to match. Flawless diamonds clustered in a semicircle, from which hung another heart-shaped gem, so dazzling that she blinked.

'Good choice,' he said on a note that made her look up sharply.

Although his eyes were hooded and unreadable, colour warmed her cheekbones and she hastily transferred her gaze back to the jewels in her hand.

Marco went on, 'The stones were chosen for their superb clarity, and I believe the tint is Silver Cape.'

'Bling indeed,' she said tonelessly and turned to the mirror, holding the earrings up to her lobes with hands that shook slightly. 'Too much, I think. The ring is enough.'

He came to stand behind her, so tall she felt small and fragile against him. The magnificent stones sparkled and shone, testament to man's desire to deck his woman with the best the world could offer. They felt heavy in her hands, and cold, as cold as the glacier-blue eyes of the man who stood looking at them.

'No, they're perfect,' he said, lips twisting in irony. 'For our purposes tonight, anyway. Stand still—I'll put them on.'

Jacoba's protest died unspoken; she stood without breathing while he slid the hooks through. His movements were deft and sure, and he smelled of soap, she realised feverishly—a citrus tang that mingled with the faint, compelling scent that was his alone, cleanly masculine, wildly exciting, and forbidden.

'There,' he said and stepped back, his face arrogant and uncompromising, the stark, autocratic framework closed against her. His eyes narrowed and he examined her with a detachment all the more chilling for being spiked by sexual awareness.

'Will I do?' she asked, and could have kicked herself for coming out with such an inane question. His sheer physical magnetism scrambled the circuits in her brain, temporarily turning her into a halfwit.

'Surely you don't need my reassurance that you look exquisite?' His smile was coolly intimidating. 'Perfect, in fact. Expensive, polished, seductive yet gracious. The dress displays every one of your considerable assets, and those diamonds will make every woman who sees you hope that if she buys the perfume some of that glamour will rub off on her. You should sell millions of litres.'

'That's why you hired me. I try to give satisfaction,' she said crisply, stupidly hurt by his tone, and walked out of the room with her head held so high it made her neck ache.

Back in the ornate saloon, she watched him pour two

glasses of champagne. For a few moments she was able to appreciate the way his austere evening clothes showed off his broad shoulders and narrow hips and long legs. Her body sprang to life, hot with a tide of desire that sang through her in an enticing flood.

Marco lifted his glass said coolly, 'Here's to triumphant success.'

Of course, he was speaking about the ad campaign! Yet something in his tone, his eyes, brought another tide of heat to her skin. She sipped the wine, pretending to savour it. 'Success,' she said neutrally. 'It's a huge gamble, though, a new perfume.'

'Indeed it is, but this one should make it. Do you like it?'

'If it's the one left in the stateroom—'

'It is,' he inserted.

'Then yes, I like it very much. What's its name?'

He shrugged. 'For some reason the publicists believe it's not a good idea to reveal that just yet. Shall we eat?'

No doubt the yacht had a dining room to match the main saloon, but they dined in a smaller, slightly more casual area. However, the expensive interior decorator who'd 'done' this yacht had stamped it with his—or her—trademark of over-the-top opulence, so that even casual meant overwhelming.

Jacoba looked at her plate with dismay; her appetite, normally hearty, had deserted her.

'Is there something wrong with the food?' Marco asked blandly.

'No, it's delicious.' She forked up a mouthful of seared tuna and forced it down her unwilling throat.

He glanced at her glass of wine, untouched except for the first sip. 'You're not drinking?'

'I rarely do,' she told him honestly. 'I don't have any head for alcohol.'

His brows lifted. 'Wise woman, then, not to try to achieve one.' He paused, before asking, 'Do you use any substitute?'

For a moment Jacoba thought she'd heard him wrong. But his formidable expression told her that, although he'd phrased it tactfully, what he'd meant was, *Do you use drugs?*

If she admitted to it, would he offer her some?

'No.' Her voice was icy with disgust.

'Good.' His eyes uncomfortably penetrating, he held her gaze for a few seconds longer than necessary.

If I had lied, she thought, he'd know.

A dangerous man...

She said thoughtfully, 'How about you?'

And was delighted when his brows shot up in unregulated surprise. However, he recovered his composure instantly. 'No,' he said on a dry note. 'I'll admit to some excess drinking when I was young and stupid at university, but that's the extent of it. I prefer my brain in its normal state.'

She nodded. 'So now that's out of the way,' she said sweetly, 'what shall we talk about?'

'You choose. Your favourite film star? Rock musician? Designer?'

He must, like so many people, think that, because she had a face the camera loved, she was shallow! Furious with him—and with herself for being upset—she told him about the book she'd just finished.

He'd read it too. And had strong ideas about it. Five minutes later she realised she was enjoying the stimulation of defending her opinions against the quick thrust of his powerful intellect.

Gradually she relaxed as they both made sure the conversation didn't veer towards the personal. He was interesting; no, more than that, he was *intriguing*, his swift, take-no-prisoners intelligence sharpening his views. She soon found herself laughing at a terse comment about a person she'd met and disliked.

Not that he was malicious, or gossiped, but he made no bones about his opinions. With him she felt exhilarated, more alive than she'd ever been, so that the strict control she'd always preserved was relaxed.

Yet all the time she was acutely, almost painfully aware of his physical charisma—the potent male grace expressed in his long, deft hands, the way white cuffs contrasted with his bronze skin, the crease of his cheeks when he laughed, the fan of unfairly long lashes across the sweeping, dramatic cheekbones…

Oh, *hell*! she thought, panicked into silence.

It wasn't fair. He was everything she should avoid—a primal threat to her peace of mind, a ruthless mogul and an Illyrian, and she wanted him so much her mouth dried and her body ached with a delicious mixture of desire and exhilarated anticipation.

He glanced at his watch and said, 'We have ten minutes before the first guests start to arrive. Do you want to freshen up?'

Jacoba seized the chance with too obvious eagerness. 'Yes, I'd better.' She scrambled to her feet.

Ever courteous, he rose at the same time, so that for a moment they faced each other like adversaries across the table.

'Not that you need it,' he said satirically, scrutinising her face. 'You've managed to eat without losing any lipstick from your perfect lips, and not a hair of that glorious red mane is out of place.'

Goaded, she said, 'I'll just check anyway. I assume you want me to wear the perfume?'

'Of course.'

Jacoba escaped, wondering what had brought an end to the stimulating companionship she'd thought they'd forged over the dinner table.

Nothing, because it had never happened. Prince Marco Considine was a clever man with superb manners and the ability to please women, and he'd managed to fool her into thinking she'd established some kind of rapport with him.

No, she'd fooled herself into thinking that.

Perhaps he'd seen what was happening, and this was his way of warning her off—a warning she shouldn't have needed.

Hot-cheeked, she added another layer of lipstick, checked her hair, ran cold water over her wrists to cool down the hectic flow of blood through her body, sprayed herself with another dose of perfume and spent three minutes doing breathing exercises.

Only then, with a smile pinned to her lips and her heart beating uncomfortably fast, did she return to the saloon.

As she came in she heard voices from the gangway. Marco took her arm. She froze, but although his hand remained, so light it was barely noticeable, a heady excitement surged through her bloodstream.

He smiled down at her, and her heart jumped while tiny febrile shivers scudded down her spine.

'You look—outrageously lovely,' he said with a raw intonation that pulled every tiny, invisible hair upright.

She hid her startled pleasure at the compliment. 'How do I smell?' And when his straight brows rose she added, 'The perfume is the whole reason for all this effort, after all.'

Those mobile brows drew together. 'Indeed it is,' he said silkily. And as voices rapidly approached, clearly about to come aboard, he commanded, 'Smile and look a little less sulky.'

Sulky! *Sulky!* She sent him a look of haughty resentment. His fingers tightened a moment on her elbow as he turned her to meet the first of the guests.

Of course, she knew many of them—the overseas VIPs were there in force, and the glitterati of New Zealand had been invited.

'I'm surprised Zoltan isn't here,' she muttered after an

actor had kissed her cheek, forgetting for a moment how furious she was with the prince.

'He'll have his hour of glory at the official launch in London,' Marco said coolly.

Four models swooped gracefully in; they spared her the usual air-kisses before eyeing Marco with lowered lashes. Impartially pleasant, he ignored their inviting glances.

He had superb manners, introducing her to the few people she didn't know, including her in the conversation—yet all the time she sensed a cool, confident possessiveness that warned off every male.

The guests made an interesting bunch, she thought ironically—some heavy-duty magnates with the current trophy wife or mistress attached like limpets, several politicians ditto, a swirl of actors and actresses, a posse of diplomats, a tenor who was setting hearts fluttering in the very best opera houses.

The last ones to arrive were a middle-aged Japanese couple, whose apology for being late was delivered with the excuse that they had been admiring bonsai trees.

'Really?' Jacoba said, returning their smiles. 'My mother adored bonsai, and had some lovely specimens.'

And wished immediately that she hadn't said anything about Ilona. Deliberately keeping her eyes on the smooth, unlined face of the woman she was talking to, she finished, 'But she was just a beginner.'

The couple beamed, and made her promise to visit their collection when next she came to their country.

'You'll have to do it,' the prince said once the Japanese couple moved on.

She sent him a cool glance. 'I plan to. They're charming.'

'Rich and influential too.'

A lift of her brows let him know she found his cynicism distasteful. 'That applies to everyone in this room, except perhaps some trophy wives. And even they might be extremely influential.'

He gave her a swift, appreciative smile that warmed her foolish heart. *'Touché.'*

A security guard appeared at the door and waited. Marco gave a swift nod. 'That's it. We're off.'

The barely noticeable hum of the engines increased, and almost immediately the yacht began to ease away from the wharf.

Jacoba hoped she might get some respite from him, but Marco had other ideas. A hand lightly touching the small of her back in an infuriatingly proprietary gesture, he steered her around with him as he moved from group to group. His tall form and handsome face would have made him impossible to overlook, but it was that intangible thing called presence that made him stand out in this collection of the powerful and the talented.

And for some reason he was determined to give the impression that they were more than business associates. Although he made her pulses soar and her blood run faster and her skin tighten in a kind of delirious anticipation, she didn't trust him.

Her refusal had been a challenge. He wanted her in his bed, and he was conducting a campaign—a clever, merciless assault on her senses, reinforcing the familiarity that a night spent dancing in his arms had produced. Her body, she thought grimly, had already capitulated; all she had for defence now was common sense and her promise to her mother.

But as the evening wore on and the moon grew larger, her fears were lulled by his charismatic impact. While she talked and laughed and listened, she found herself swaying towards him quite naturally, her spirits building in the addictive, intoxicating charm of his attention.

When the yacht turned and began to make its way back to the harbour she was still by his side. She said, 'I'll be back shortly.'

He gave her a swift glance, shocked her by nodding, and turned back to the man he was talking to.

That swift inclination of his black head had been permission to leave him! Fuming, she made her way towards the cloakroom.

Who the hell did he think he was—arrogant, overbearing bastard? He'd monopolised her all evening and she'd let him! And, more humiliating than that, she'd been thoroughly enjoying herself.

The cloakroom was almost empty except for a woman she recognised as being attached to a property developer. She gave Jacoba a dismissive nod, but was still carefully delineating her plump, perfect lips when Jacoba emerged from the stall.

The woman slid her lipstick into her tiny, jewelled bag, and said, 'Are those diamonds real?'

Startled, Jacoba prevaricated, 'I didn't ask. Why?'

The woman gave a mocking grin. 'Can't be, or we'd have the security guard in here with us. They look good, though. You're doing quite well for yourself, aren't you?' And when Jacoba gave her a blank look, she elaborated, 'You've got the prince on a string, and he's got the world at his fingertips. Just remember, though, the guy's not noted for long relationships. So get what you can from him, and make sure it's safe in the bank where he can't lay hands on it.'

'Thank you,' Jacoba said politely, drying her hands. The heart-shaped diamond caught on the towel; she looked at it and for some stupid reason her eyes began to fill.

'And whatever you do, don't go thinking he's in love with you,' the woman said harshly. 'Men like him don't marry women like us.'

Jacoba stared at her. 'I don't—' she began, only to be interrupted.

'I've been watching you; you're falling for him. Hell, I don't blame you—he's too good to be true! And I can see you don't believe me, but it's the truth. Men like him use us, pay for it, and then when they're sick of us they throw us on the scrapheap.'

She walked out of the room, leaving Jacoba feeling horribly sorry for her. No matter what she was now, once she'd been young and in love and it had rebounded on her, hurting her so much she'd given advice to a woman she didn't even know.

Good advice, but quite unnecessary.

Because of course Jacoba didn't believe that Marco was in love with her. And she wasn't falling in love with *him*.

On the way back she was waylaid by a journalist who wrote a gossip column in the latest, sexiest, most hip magazine in New Zealand. Or so its publicity said; certainly many people feared Gregory Border.

Jacoba knew why. Although a couple of years previously she'd been perfectly polite when she refused his suggestion of an affair, her rebuff had clearly stung, because since then she'd been fodder for his particular brand of retaliation.

'You look fantastic,' he said, his smile showing his teeth. 'And is that delicious fragrance the scent that all the fuss is about?'

Did Marco want this generally known? Jacoba produced a wide-eyed glance and a smile. 'I don't know,' she said serenely.

He leaned forward and picked up her hand, dragging it up to his mouth in spite of her resistance so that he could pretend to kiss the vulnerable underside of her wrist. Her other hand formed into a fist, but she couldn't hit him in the solar plexus, not here. And he knew it.

'Mmm,' he murmured. 'Just a little too heavy on the boudoir for my liking, which is rather ironic when it's generally known that apart from your usual partner you're pretty much an ice queen. What does the forceful Hawke think of the thing you have going with the prince?'

'No comment,' she said, each syllable coated with ice. 'Let me go. If you touch me again I'll have you arrested for assault.'

'You wouldn't dare—'

'I would,' a deep, iron-hard voice interrupted from behind her.

Gregory Border dropped her hand as though it burnt.

Intense relief surged through Jacoba, followed by a sense of dread. The prince must walk like a cat—and when she turned he was watching the other man with the menacing intentness of a predator.

'You don't have to worry,' the journalist said, an unbecoming tinge of colour across his cheeks. 'We're old friends, aren't we, Jacoba?'

'So why did she tell you to let her hand go?'

'Perhaps she's worried about the rock she's wearing on her finger,' Border said, his tone halfway between a sneer and bitter envy. 'But I don't steal.'

Only reputations, Jacoba thought scornfully. Marco's silence was somehow more ominous than anything he could have said.

The journalist looked from Jacoba to the prince's intimidating face, and shrugged. 'Now that I'm here, is there any chance of an interview?' He looked back at Jacoba. 'Singly? Or together?'

'No,' Marco said with chilling dispassion. 'Not now, not ever. And in future, keep your hands to yourself.'

Border shrugged. 'Can't blame a man for trying,' he said on a would-be jaunty note, but his glance at Jacoba promised retribution.

'I can.'

Jacoba shivered. Marco didn't have to threaten; he spoke with the complete assurance of a man who knew he could accomplish whatever he set out to do.

CHAPTER SIX

AFTER a short, tense silence the journalist gave another shrug and stepped back. 'Then I'll just have to make do with what I've got,' he said significantly, and let his gaze rest a moment on Jacoba's calm face.

Shivering, she caught a flash of reckless triumph in his smile.

Although Marco recognised the threat, now wasn't the time to call him on it. But then the bastard wouldn't have made it if he hadn't guessed that he'd be safe.

Ignoring him, the prince smiled down at Jacoba. 'We should mingle,' he said, and walked her away.

When they were out of Border's hearing, she muttered in a worried voice, 'He's a gossip columnist—most people try to keep on his right side because he's good at sniffing out dirt. And he's hugely popular amongst the set that spends money. It's not wise to cross him; he makes a dangerous enemy.'

'So,' Marco said with a cool lack of emphasis, 'do I.'

He wasn't going to tell her that, however powerful Border thought himself, his fate had been sealed the second Marco had looked up and seen him kissing Jacoba's hand.

The rush of fierce, mindless jealousy had startled—no, hell, it had *shocked* him.

He didn't get jealous. He'd never had to. And because

pragmatism told him that his success with women almost certainly owed a lot to his name and his money and the title—plus the excellent genes that had bequeathed him his face and body—he didn't consider himself spoilt. But he'd never wanted a woman he couldn't have.

There was a first time for everything, he thought grimly, and no doubt it was long overdue for him. He glanced down at Jacoba's serene, exquisite face.

Only it wasn't so serene now; she was looking at him with furrowed brows. He had to stop himself from kissing the concern away.

The swift, unbidden desire to protect her both astonished and infuriated him. It was more dangerous and unexpected than the jealousy. She wasn't a social butterfly, but he'd seen her occasionally across various crowded rooms, sometimes with Hawke Kennedy, more often without. He'd known he could want her, but because he'd liked Kennedy he'd never made any move on her.

But now everything had changed; he'd seen her swift unbidden response to his touch, felt her mouth soften under his, and he'd been appalled at the amount of effort it took him to pull away from her.

Tonight he'd deliberately given the impression that they were a couple. He'd told himself it was to set off that precious buzz, the intangible air of expectancy that built into interest and publicity. Properly managed, some of the gloss and mystique of occasions such as this would rub off on the woman in the street, the mythical entity who'd decide whether the perfume became a lifelong commitment or ended up as a fly-by-night affair.

But that hadn't been the reason he'd kept Jacoba beside him all evening; put brutally, he couldn't help himself. Another ruthless surge of appetite sliced through Marco's will-power like a sword through silk. She had the power to make him revert to type, like those hard-bitten ancestors whose portraits lined the walls in the castle they'd lived in and raided from.

Inclination warred with his upbringing. He was a civilised modern man, not some warrior prince from the Middle Ages; women had a perfect right to say no without being badgered.

But he wanted him; every male instinct in his body told him that.

Jacoba's eyes widened and she glanced away, a faint flush showing along her magnificent cheekbones. 'He doesn't like me,' she said, so quietly he could barely hear her, 'so I'm afraid you won't get good publicity from him.'

'You know the old adage,' Marco told her on a cynical note. 'Any publicity is better than none. And if he doesn't like you, why was he kissing your hand?'

'A power play.' Her voice was restrained and remote.

Blood rushed to Marco's head again. For an unguarded moment he found himself wishing he'd followed his first basic instinct and hit the hack on his jaw—a primitive response he despised.

Jacoba Sinclair, with her patrician beauty and that hair like a river of dark fire, was getting to him in a way no other woman had. He could try to convince himself that it was purely physical; that was certainly part of it, but he'd enjoyed her mind too, relishing her sharp observations as they'd eaten dinner.

She was an enigma. Behind that reserved façade he sensed something hidden, reserves she kept carefully secret.

Not caring about the abruptness of his tone, he said, 'Why don't you like him?'

An undernote to the words—colder than steel and every bit as hard—warned Jacoba to be diplomatic. Flippantly, she said, 'For the best reason in the world—because he doesn't like me.'

'The truth,' Marco commanded, still in that forbidding tone.

She looked up, met eyes of uncompromising blue.

'I don't like lies,' he said.

'And I don't like being badgered when it's nothing to do with you.'

'Nothing to do with me personally, maybe,' he said, his voice as inflexible as his expression, 'but the success of this campaign largely depends on you. If he's likely to try derailing it, I need to know. You said he's good at sniffing out dirt; if he's got any information that would show you in a bad light, tell me now.'

'He has none.'

Marco believed her. 'Then what is it?'

After a rapid glance at his arrogant face, Jacoba chose to give him a modified version of the truth. 'He tried to get me into bed. When I said no, he decided to teach me a lesson.'

Marco's black brows met in a ruthless line. 'Don't tell me he conducts a feud with every woman who turns him down!'

Hiding the slight shiver his choice of words caused, she said, 'I don't know. Possibly.'

He said something in Illyrian that startled her. 'So he's a blackmailer. At least you didn't give in to him.' And after a silent second he drawled, 'I assume you didn't.'

The lazy, cool comment was underpinned by an implacable note that sent another chilly shiver over Jacoba's skin.

'Of course I didn't,' she said briskly, not looking at him.

Even if she'd found Border attractive, she'd have rejected him; he'd sickened her by telling her he didn't mind sharing her with Hawke.

Assuming a light note, she went on, 'It's an occupational hazard. Most men can take no for an answer, but some turn ugly.'

'Does he harass you?' Marco asked, his voice a low growl.

She looked at him ironically. 'Not now, and no more than some others.'

'If he tries anything, let me know.'

The cold determination in his voice, in his expression, revealed that he meant what he said. Clearly his possessiveness was tempered by a protective instinct a mile wide.

'I can cope,' she said forthrightly. 'As I said, it goes with the territory. Models are often considered fair game.'

His eyes narrowed and behind the superbly classical features she glimpsed the inherent strength of the man, a formidable authority based on rock-hard integrity. He set his own standards, she thought, and lived by them, no matter how difficult they might make his life.

'I want to know,' he repeated. 'While you're doing this campaign you're my responsibility.'

She gave a slight shrug. 'I'm my own responsibility. Border was just being a jerk.'

'Will he hound you in his column?'

This time her shrug was a bit deeper. 'Probably. It doesn't mean anything; in New Zealand everyone recognises everyone else, is fully aware of their business. If they don't know why he makes snide comments about me, they can guess. It's no big deal, and he knows it. Even though he relishes his little bit of power, he must find it frustrating that no one outside New Zealand reads his column.' She sent him a satirical glance. 'And New Zealand is a tiny market compared to even Australia. His sniping won't make much difference to the ultimate sales of the perfume.'

The prince demanded arrogantly, 'Why doesn't Kennedy stop him?'

Jacoba lifted her brows. 'Hawke knows I can look after myself. I'm not afraid of Border—nothing he can do will hurt me, Mar—' She stopped, her tongue tangling in her mouth.

His eyes gleamed. 'You were about to say my name,' he invited courteously.

'I don't know whether I should call you whatever it is princes get called in your country,' she said, stupidly prim.

He told her his designation in Illyrian. 'Your Highness, in other words,' he said in English. 'But friends use my given name.'

'I don't know the ins and outs of protocol,' she evaded, wondering why pronouncing his name felt like a symbolic surrender.

'So say it.' He delivered the command in a tone soft enough to be heard only by them.

'Your Highness. Marco.' The syllables rolled fluidly off her tongue, and she found herself absurdly wishing that she could simply relate to him as a man.

But she couldn't. Although he didn't know it, they were both linked and separated by a heritage that had always been a frightening mystery to her.

He said, 'You could almost be Illyrian, the way you pronounce the vowel sounds.'

Panic gripped her in talons of iron. She had to drag breath into starving lungs before she could say, 'It must be because I grew up with French as a second language.'

'Possibly,' he said, but his eyes were keen, and she wondered frantically if she'd turned pale.

Abruptly conscious that they were the objects of covert scrutiny by quite a few of the guests, she said unevenly, 'We'd better start circulating again.'

He nodded and took her arm, turning her to face the crowd in a gesture that was as obvious as it was deliberate.

Jacoba caught the journalist's eye, and lifted her chin at his malicious smile. Let him say what he liked in his column; she had more to worry about than his barbed comments.

By the time the yacht had tied up at the wharf again and the last guests had left, Jacoba felt as though she'd been pummelled with hammers all night. Yet weariness couldn't dim the exhilarating anticipation that still burned brightly within her.

'Tired?' Marco enquired as he showed her to the stateroom where her clothes waited. She'd already stripped off the jewellery and handed it to the security guard, who'd carried it away, no doubt into an armoured vehicle.

'A little,' she agreed.

'I'm sorry this came after a day spent shooting, but the publicity people were very eager to use you when they discovered you were going to be in Auckland today.' He looked down at her. 'Do you want to walk back to the hotel once you've changed, or would you rather I order a taxi?'

'Walk.' The yacht was moored at the Viaduct Basin, only a few hundred metres from the hotel she was staying in.

Without preamble, Marco said, 'I'm leaving the country tomorrow.'

Disappointment—keen as a blade—shattered the fragile bubble of her pleasure. She should be relieved. When this temporary madness had left her, she would be.

But at the moment she could only stifle a shattering sense of loss.

So she was rather proud of the cool interest in her tone when she asked, 'Back to Illyria?'

'Via America.' He sent her a glance. 'Come with me.'

'No,' she said instantly, but she wanted to—oh, how she wanted to! She just didn't dare.

But Marco knew. His smile hardened. 'Why not surrender now and save yourself a lot of angst?' he suggested, his idle tone contrasting spectacularly with his narrow-eyed scrutiny.

Jacoba threw him a proud glance. 'I don't do surrender,' she said sweetly.

One night-dark brow lifted in sardonic, deeply subversive

appreciation. He opened the door into the stateroom, standing back to let her into the fragile safety of the room.

'Mutual surrender is no loss of pride,' he said, and before she could answer he closed the door and left her alone.

As she slipped the silk dress from her tense body and hung it up, as she pulled on her jeans and T-shirt and replaced the high-heeled sandals with her sensible flat shoes, Jacoba ached with the hungry passion that had been building all evening.

Why shouldn't she have a wild affair with him? Most of her friends wouldn't think twice.

But then, none of her friends had a past so shrouded in mystery that all she really knew about it was her father's death and her mother's terror of the secret police.

No. Even if she was prepared to risk it, there was Lexie to consider. Firming her lips, she left the stateroom, her shoulders and spine very straight, her determination screwed up to its highest pitch.

Marco had changed too, into a black shirt and narrow-cut black trousers. In them he looked lethal, like some forbidding denizen of the darkness.

This time, instead of taking her arm, he offered his. She hesitated, then put her hand through it, almost shuddering at the pleasure of his body heat.

'Are you cold?' He knew she wasn't.

'Not at all,' she returned politely. 'It seems that we're in for an early summer.'

'What are your plans for the season?'

'Oh, work.' She kept her words light, deliberately vague. 'And there are all the parties for the launch.'

The area was humming with people in the bars and restaurants, many taking a lively interest in the tall couple walking along the street. Recognising her, one group of young men sitting outside a bar called out; they weren't a threat, merely cheeky. She smiled, but kept walking, conscious of Marco shepherding her like some big, subtly menacing, totally competent guard dog.

'I'd like to see you again before they start,' Marco said quietly.

Tension spiralled out of control between them. Jacoba almost flinched when he continued, 'And not in a business sense.'

Perilous joy fountained up through her, warm and sweet as a summer night, filling her with delight. She swallowed and steeled herself. 'I'm afraid that's not a good idea.'

'Why?' Marco said relentlessly. 'Because of Hawke Kennedy?'

Jacoba hesitated again. *Lie*, common sense urged.

Because even if a relationship with Marco weren't too dangerous to consider, it wouldn't last. The woman in the cloakroom had been right; men like the prince didn't marry women like her. When the time came he'd choose someone with the right bloodlines.

Marry? Where the hell had that thought come from? Some stupidly romantic part of her she'd kept hidden until now...

She stole another glance at Marco, an unregenerate part of her wishing fiercely that he'd sweep her off her feet and into a passionate encounter that would make saying yes much easier. Although she respected him for refusing to use sex to persuade her, she was faintly chilled by his matter-of-fact attitude.

Their eyes met. Heat kindled in the pale depths of his, transfixing her. Any suspicions of a pragmatic approach vanished and her heart began its familiar thudding while sensation coursed through her in a tingling, tumbling flood, hot and sweet and sensuous.

Yes, she thought with a sudden, swift jolt of triumphant recognition, this is what I want. *He* is what I want.

And she could never have him.

Yet she couldn't lie to him. 'Hawke is my dearest friend,' she said. 'When I started modelling I was only sixteen— green as grass and without any conception of just how predatory some men could be. My agency was protective, but Hawke stood as a sort of sponsor.' She shrugged. 'He already had a name as someone to watch out for, and when I shamelessly used his name and influence, men backed off.'

'And he was happy to be used like that?'

She moved her shoulders uneasily. Not that there was anything to gather from his tone—in fact, its studied neutrality jolted her already heightened senses into full alert.

'I don't think he saw it as being used,' she said quietly.

Marco nodded. 'And I suppose the accepted tale of you being lovers was a cover for any real relationships you had.'

Only two, and neither had been serious. Her background had made her too reserved, too careful to open herself to any lover.

Anyway, compared to Hawke most men seemed curiously lacking in vitality.

But not Marco, she thought with a skip of her heart. He could more than hold his own in the vitality stakes! She said colourlessly, 'Yes.'

'So are you in any relationship now?' He spoke formally, but there was no mistaking his tone. He was determined to know.

'No,' she said automatically.

'Neither am I.'

She knew that. Since he'd taken over his cousin's software empire, combining it with his own far from insignificant enterprises, he'd been working too hard to be able to maintain a love affair. During the past couple of years even the tabloids had given up on him.

But Jacoba read the business pages; the immense task of

consolidation had almost finished. Perhaps he felt he could take a breather now.

Perhaps she was a little light relief, a reward for all his hard work?

Dismayed at how strongly she resisted this thought, she set her jaw. 'It doesn't make any difference,' she said, but her voice—tinged by yearning—gave her away.

Marco's gaze lingered on her mouth. 'So we have tonight,' he said softly, his voice deep and dangerously compelling.

That burnished gaze fired Jacoba's reckless need into the stratosphere. Summoning all her will to resist the adrenalin rush of temptation, she fought back words of surrender. 'No, we *don't*.' But the strain showed in her ragged tone. 'I'm not inviting you in.'

She was fighting a rearguard action, and he knew it. In their world people took lovers and discarded them without worrying about morality. He might start to wonder what reason she might have to refuse him. And if he did, he might search for reasons…

'I'm staying there too.'

Unsteadily she muttered, 'How convenient.'

He paused before saying with a dry intonation, 'I own it.'

'Ah, I see.' She took a shallow breath. 'So do I, in a way— I have shares in the company. Tell me, is it true you're planning to set up a luxury hotel in the Bay of Islands?'

'My board is considering it,' he said, his interest piqued.

She looked ethereal, a woman of fire and gossamer sensuality, far too beautiful to take seriously except as a lover, yet she was no fool. Her conversation over dinner had shown that she read widely, and she had a thorough knowledge of politics and world affairs, as well as the stock market.

Although she'd be beautiful until the day she died—her superb skin and that elegant bone structure would see to that—

she was astute enough to realise that her career wasn't going to last forever, and to take steps to ensure a solid future.

Hawke Kennedy's influence, possibly. That thought produced a now familiar stab of jealousy.

Made wary by his silence, Jacoba plodded on, 'You'll have a fight on your hands. The locals are very suspicious of any development that might compromise the beauty of the bay.'

'I don't mind fair fights. And I think we can convince them that instead of detracting from the area's beauty, we'll be enhancing it.'

He guided her past a group whose loud laughter and clumsy gestures indicated they'd had too much to drink. One or two catcalls revealed that she'd been recognised again, but they died immediately. Jacoba didn't fool herself that her carefully blank face had shut them up. Marco's readiness to intervene charged the air around them, and although they were outnumbered she felt utterly secure.

A few steps on he said, 'Besides, I understand their concerns. I am not an insensitive developer.'

They turned into the entrance of the hotel, and she slid her hand from his arm. 'If your board is planning anything like this hotel, not many people in the bay will object.'

It breasted onto the harbour, as sleekly elegant as a liner, its proportions fitting into the panorama of low volcanoes and headlands that made the Auckland waterfront.

As they went up in the private lift that serviced the suites, he said, 'Thank you. You did very well tonight, but was I right in suspecting that you do not enjoy parties?'

'Usually I enjoy them very much,' she said, her brows drawing together.

'So what was wrong with tonight?'

When she didn't answer, he turned her face so that he could read it.

His long index finger smoothed away the frown. 'I know what was wrong,' he said, his voice deep and sure and sexy, a slight smile not softening the hard line of his mouth.

He would always be a buccaneer, she thought wistfully, her mouth trembling as that knowing finger stroked the length of it. Even now, with passion glittering in the crystalline depths of his eyes, he looked more like a conqueror than a lover.

For a moment she was gripped by panic. What the hell was she *doing*? She hardly knew him! Yet dancing with him in the restaurant overlooking the mountains had forged a need that had grown uncontrollably.

His kisses and caresses had boosted that intense physical knowledge, sharpened it, honing it into recklessness. A shiver of anticipation worked its way through her.

His finger dropped from her mouth. He picked her up and said gutturally, 'Open the door.'

Weak with longing, she obeyed, and he carried her into the suite, then stopped and looked around, making a rough sound of satisfaction when he saw the sofa.

'Good, a decent-sized piece of furniture,' he said, his voice edged with hunger.

But once he'd sat down he held her against him, his cheek against her forehead as if for the moment that simple contact satisfied a longing he hadn't recognised until then. The last shreds of Jacoba's resistance died. In his arms she felt totally, wonderfully safe…

In a voice harsh with hunger, he said, 'Look at me.'

Jacoba's eyes devoured the tough, autocratic contours of his face, the mellow combination of olive skin and night-dark hair, sparked by his arctic gaze.

'How the hell do you do that?'

'Do what?' she asked, genuinely surprised.

His laugh was short and self-derisory. 'Burn me with a

glance,' he told her. 'Grey eyes are usually cool and clear and translucent, but yours are smoky and seductive and tantalising. They drive me mad.'

Ruthlessly stopping any reply with another kiss, he found the soft swell of her breast with his seeking hand. Sensations met and warred in her—the open conquest of the deep kiss, and the tide of glittering provocation as his fingers cupped and stroked her.

She pressed her hands on each side of his face, the slight friction of his beard adding yet another layer to her response. Fearlessly she met his narrow-eyed scrutiny, crystalline and compelling as diamonds, but the struggle to control her inner wildness threatened to overwhelm her.

Incredulously she realised that he too was fighting that battle. She saw the moment his control snapped and the dark fire of need overwhelmed him. Yet he kissed the line of her jaw with wonderful gentleness, and then down her throat, his mouth lingering with exquisite precision on certain spots as though he knew by instinct how to arouse her.

A little whimper broke from her throat; she ran one hand through the black silk of his hair, its virile, springy texture yet another aphrodisiac. Her heart was pounding so much it threatened to deafen her, and she couldn't think. Although she knew in some recess in her mind that she shouldn't be doing this, she couldn't remember why or how something so foolish as restraint should be necessary.

'Will I spoil this pretty thing if I rip it from you?' he asked, the wry humour in his voice sending a thrill of craving through her.

'Yes, so in return you'll have to let me tear your shirt from you,' she said, her voice so low and husky and teasing she didn't recognise it. 'Fair's fair, after all.'

Eyes gleaming, he laughed deep in his throat and leaned

back against the sofa, letting his hands lie along the back. 'Feel free,' he invited, his smile crooked.

She released the hem of his black shirt from his trousers, heard his sharply indrawn breath, and looked up with a question in her eyes.

'Hell, but you're beautiful,' he said gutturally, and she noticed that the muscles in his arms were bulging with the effort to stay still.

Sheer mischievous joy surged through her. A smile curving lips already tender from his kisses, she flipped the shirt over his head. He released his death grip on the sofa and let her undo the buttons at his cuffs.

He wore a rollneck jersey beneath, its fine texture clinging lovingly to every line of his torso, revealing the powerful contours—and the sharp rise and fall of his chest as he fought to control his breathing.

'You bought some merino-wool clothes while you were in the South Island,' she breathed, and stroked the dark material with a tentative finger.

His eyes smouldered and the muscles along his strong jaw tightened as he said something in the language she barely recognised as Illyrian.

It was an oath, a quiet imprecation calling for strength; she'd heard her mother use it occasionally when she and her sister were being particularly trying.

Mama, she thought desperately—Mama…

She closed her eyes and muttered hoarsely, 'I can't—don't want this.'

After a moment of stark tension he said brutally, 'You're lying. You want me as much as I want you.'

Swift, hot colour burned along her high, sculpted cheekbones. After a tense moment she got her thoughts into sufficient order to mutter, 'That isn't the point.'

The intoxicating rush of adrenalin had ebbed, leaving her cold and shaky. Taking him by surprise, she scrambled off his knee.

Her legs shook; he'd be furious and she didn't blame him, but at least she'd come to her senses while they still had on most of their clothes, she thought wildly.

Bolstering her courage, she turned and faced him, her head flung back and her chin angled in what she hoped would look like arrogance.

He was already on his feet. Her heart quailed; big and dark and dominating in the sleekly impersonal sitting room, he was watching her with a face entirely devoid of expression.

Yet she could feel the force of the emotions he'd leashed behind those hard, inscrutable features.

She swallowed and said, 'I'm sorry.' Her voice sounded thin and wooden, as though she were repeating something learned by rote. 'That was unforgivable of me. I don't—I don't want this, Marco.'

One black brow climbed in sardonic comment. 'You need to work on those mixed messages,' he said courteously.

He was right, damn him, but it was like a slap in the face. While frustrated passion rioted through her, he could make a comment that showed he wasn't badly upset. Although his crystalline gaze never left her face and she was uneasily aware of that brilliant, formidable brain working, he seemed unperturbed.

She bit her lip, releasing it when she saw his icy blue eyes note the small betraying gesture. 'I'm sorry,' she said, more strongly this time. She clenched her hands into fists at her sides.

Do it, the stern voice of duty told her. *Tell him to go*.

Aloud, she said starkly, 'I don't want an affair with you.'

'Why?'

Oh, God, why couldn't he just accept it and go? She had no sensible answer that wouldn't give too much away. He knew she went up in flames in his arms.

When she didn't answer, he said with the steely civility she found so intimidating, 'Your response seemed genuine enough. Or are you that good an actress?'

Desperate to make an end of it, she blurted, 'I'd prefer it if we kept our relationship on a purely business footing.'

When he inclined his head, she saw the prince in action— formidably polite, authoritative and totally intimidating. 'Or have I misread the situation?' he asked coolly. 'I prefer plain speaking, and although you seem to find it difficult to actually tell me, you must. How much will it cost me?'

CHAPTER SEVEN

'WHAT?' Jacoba blinked, then caught his meaning. Anger flooded her skin with heat that drained away into a bitter humiliation. 'If you mean what I think you mean, I am not a prostitute,' she said abruptly, fighting back the lump that threatened to block her throat.

'Of course you're not, but it's only sensible of you to establish your conditions before you get too involved.' Marco's smile cut through her like tempered steel. 'I very much enjoyed the sample of your skills that we've shared so far. I'm quite ready to buy.'

She faced him, two spots of colour burning in her cheeks. 'I've been insulted by experts,' she said unevenly, 'but none quite as good as you. Please go.'

'Certainly.' He slung the shirt she'd taken off him over one shoulder and strolled out towards the door.

Unwillingly she watched him, welcoming the anger and hurt that soothed her desolation. He walked easily, completely at home, moving with the lithe freedom of a predator.

At the door he turned and examined her. 'I'll see you again shortly. I hope you haven't forgotten when we're launching the perfume.'

'No,' she said colourlessly. 'It's in my diary.'

His smile didn't reach his cold, unsparing eyes. 'See that you turn up,' he advised, and swung around and left.

She locked the door after him, then sank down into a chair and shivered, rubbing her upper arms to try and bring some warmth into her body.

This couldn't be heartbreak—but oh, it felt like it!

Closing her eyes, she tried to block out the prospect of the immediate future, when she'd be faced with meeting him at various functions and enduring the freezing contempt in his eyes, knowing what he thought of her.

Well, it couldn't be anything worse than her opinion of him, she thought valiantly, trying to whip up that righteous anger again. He had the gall, the utter cheek, to despise *her* when he'd been quite ready to *pay* for her sexual services.

Disgusting.

But it wasn't disgust that brought painful tears to her eyes and kept her awake for most of the night.

The next morning, showered and dressed, cosmetics applied to hide the ravages of the night, Jacoba walked into the sitting room of the suite to the sound of a discreet knock. Crazy anticipation set her heart drumming so heavily when she opened the door.

But it wasn't Marco. Instead, she saw the butler standing there with a huge basket of flowers.

'Madam,' he said formally, proffering them.

She took them, noting the Peruvian lilies, a red so dark and deep it matched her hair. Her foolish heart contracted; surely the colour meant Marco had chosen them himself, not merely phoned an order through? Or were they just another, more subtle insult—payment for those 'samples of her skills' he'd been so scathing about?

The butler held out an envelope and the complimentary

newspaper. 'These also,' he said with a smile. 'Is there anything I can get for you?'

'No, thank you.' Once the door was closed she put the flowers onto a table, then stood looking foolishly down at the envelope. Although it had nothing but her name on it in strong black writing, she knew immediately who had written the salutation.

Biting her lip, she read the message. Brief and oddly formal, it was certainly noncommittal, she thought cynically. It could never be used as evidence!

I will contact you in London when you get back.

He'd signed it with a simple initial M.

Shakily she crumpled the sheet of paper and threw it into a rubbish bin, but almost immediately she retrieved it, smoothing out the creases with a twisted smile that mocked her desire for this one, tiny souvenir.

Although the thought of food nauseated her, she ordered fruit and muesli and some coffee, then sat down to calm her mind by reading the paper.

On the back page her eyes fell on the gossip column, noting her name amidst the print. Her heart dropped and she felt sick, but she forced herself to read it, disgust stiffening her features. How could anyone manage to make an evening reception on a yacht sound like a sordid commercial transaction?

Because Gregory Border had a sordid mind, she thought angrily.

And he wasn't the only one.

But it was the last sentence that drove the colour from her skin.

It's been whispered that the prince and our favourite model have more than a contract in common—and although I know what you're thinking, I'm not referring to that, either! In spite of her impeccably Celtic name, the beautiful model is rumoured to have strong family links to Illyria.

'Oh, God!' she whispered, bolting to her feet.

She stared around, then drew in a gasping breath and forced her frantic mind to slow down, to think logically. Almost certainly she had no need to panic, because—surely?—whatever her mother feared had died with the dictator.

She needed to discuss this with someone who wasn't emotionally caught up in the situation. Hawke…

She sat down and rang a car-hire firm.

By the time she reached the Bay of Islands she was hot, and she'd managed to spill a glass of orange juice down the front of her T-shirt. Although Hawke wasn't home, his car was in the garage, so she let herself in with her key and decided to change before she tracked him down.

She'd just showered the sticky juice off when she heard movement in the front of the house. A wry smile lifted the corners of her mouth. Damn, why couldn't she fall in love with him instead of loving him with the steady affection of a sister? It would make life so much simpler.

She shrugged herself into her wrap and went to let him know she was there, pushing open the door to say, 'Darling, thank heavens—'

Unfortunately he wasn't alone. And from the momentary expression on his face, she realised she was most emphatically not welcome! In fact, he'd thrust the woman with him behind his big body, as though to protect her.

He's in love! she thought, surprisingly dismayed.

'Jacoba,' he said levelly. 'What the hell are you doing here?'

'Oh, sorry.' His tone hurt, and in spite of herself she felt a pang of anxiety. Keeping her voice light and pleasant she said, 'Darling, I know I'm a day or so too early. I didn't realise that you had visitors.'

'Only one,' Hawke said easily, once more fully in control.

In a level, ironic voice he introduced them—Jacoba as an old friend, and his lover by name.

Jacoba's lashes drooped to hide her shock. The woman was Princess Melissa Considine. Marco's younger sister.

Of all the *horrible* coincidences…

After a frozen moment she gave her head a tiny shake and let her expression relax into a smile, hoping fervently that neither Hawke nor his lover had noticed. He deserved to be happy, and there was nothing to stop *him* from achieving it.

With stilted politeness she and Melissa Considine went through the greeting routine. The princess's tangled honey-dark hair and flushed, exquisite skin combined with the sensuous contours of her mouth to tell Jacoba what had been happening. They'd made love down there on the beach.

A few minutes later, when Hawke showed her into her bedroom, she said contritely, 'Sorry, sorry, sorry! I should have let you know I'd be early. I'll eat in my room tonight.'

'Don't be an idiot,' he told her, but his tone revealed that Melissa Considine was important to him.

'She believes we're lovers,' Jacoba stated.

'Why did you come today?'

Torn, she looked at him sideways. He said, 'Tell me, Jake. I can see you're in trouble.'

'Not exactly.' But because the habits of a lifetime were hard to resist, she told him what had happened. He knew about their mother's fear of being hunted down by the secret police, but his green eyes narrowed when she revealed the gossip columnist's bolt out of the blue.

Hawke surveyed her face with an intent gaze that saw too much. 'You're in love with that bloody prince,' he said softly.

Jacoba shook her head vigorously. 'I don't believe in love at first sight.'

'Neither did I.'

She gave him a dazzling smile and a swift, fervent hug. 'It's about time! So now go and make sure Melissa understands she has nothing to worry about.'

'If she doesn't accept my word that we're not lovers, *she* isn't worth worrying about,' he said uncompromisingly.

Jacoba jeered, 'Most people would believe you really mean that, but I know better.'

He tugged a lock of her wet hair. 'You know me too well. Do you want me to force Border to print a retraction?'

'Could you?'

He shrugged. 'I could try.'

'No,' she said, frowning. 'You'd only make him dig deeper. I really wanted to ask you if you thought Lexie and I have any reason to worry about being outed as Illyrians. Now I've just made things bad for you.'

'It hasn't helped,' he conceded, 'but I know what I want and I'll get it in the end. As for worrying about anyone knowing you're Illyrian by birth—God knows what your mother went through before she got to New Zealand. Whatever happened, she didn't dare accept you were safe here, so she did a good job of frightening you both into silence. You don't just brush that sort of thing off, but I'm sure that if she'd still been alive when Paulo Considine died she'd have realised she no longer needed to be afraid.'

Eating her dinner in her room that night with a pretend headache, Jacoba wondered if the blood feuds their mother had talked of could have been a reason for her mother's fear, but it didn't make sense. Even if they still happened, Ilona had been the victim, not the aggressor.

Jacoba had hoped her absence would give Hawke a chance

to make up with his lover, but the next morning it was obvious things weren't going well. Although the princess had exquisite manners, she was cool and remote, and Hawke's tension was apparent to Jacoba—although perhaps not to Melissa Considine, who was flying back to Illyria that morning.

Jacoba met Hawke at the door when he arrived back from the airport. He'd always been there for her, a steady rock in her life, but he had other loyalties now.

He took in her hire car, packed and ready to go. 'What are you doing?'

'I had no right to inflict myself on you,' she said, and smiled mistily at him. 'I've used you for years, and it's time it stopped. Besides, you're going after her, aren't you?'

His grim, narrow smile told her she'd guessed right. 'I'll give her a few days,' he said. 'As for using me—don't be an idiot. But it probably is time we moved on.'

Her eyes filled with tears. 'Yes,' she said simply. 'Thanks, Hawke. I have no right to ask you, but—would you mind not telling the princess about us—about the Illyrian connection? It's not just my secret. There's Lexie; I rang her last night, and she's still twitchy about being Illyrian.'

'Of course I won't tell Melissa,' he said brusquely. 'What are you going to do?'

She'd wanted to call in and see Lexie, but her sister had vetoed that idea; she was just heading off for a tour of the Outback. 'I'll go back to London and organise myself into retirement. And then I'll come back.'

'Are you still keen on writing that novel?'

'Yes,' she said, although her ambition seemed faded and distant, as though Marco had somehow managed to push everything in her life into the background.

Hawke surprised her with a kiss on her cheek. 'Then consider what you're going through to be raw material,' he said. 'But—a word about Marco Considine. He might be hard to shake off. He knows what he wants.'

Jacoba shrugged, tension pooling beneath her ribs. 'It's all right—once I've fulfilled my obligation in the launch of this perfume, I'll come back home and never see him again.'

Jacoba closed the little telephone with a snap, hoping that this time her agent realised it was no use dangling ever more lucrative contracts in front of her.

She'd been in London for four days, seeing no one while she'd made plans and set about organising her future. Perhaps she should thank Marco—if he hadn't chosen her for the campaign she might have gone on like this for years, wasting time until eventually no one wanted her in front of a camera...

No, she thought sturdily, the past years hadn't been wasted. She'd met some wonderful people—creative, passionate, dedicated to fashion. But her passion, her creativity and dedication had never been used, and over the past few years she'd become aware of a growing dissatisfaction. So it was making Marco too important to believe he'd produced such a change in her.

Her telephone summoned her again. She picked it up. 'Hello.'

'Jacoba.'

Marco's voice. Her heart leapt in her chest—a real physical movement, she thought dazedly, pressing a hand over it.

With a struggle she managed to control her tone, to tune it so that her words sounded almost amused. 'This is a surprise, Your Highness.'

'Last time we met you called me by my name,' he drawled, his voice low and intimate with an undertone of raw hunger that sent fiery little shafts right through her, tangling her thoughts and reducing her to a creature of sensation.

No, she thought bleakly, forcing herself to reimpose some sort of tenuous control. Once bitten, twice shy. 'Where are you?'

'On the street outside your door.'

Pulses thudding, she cast an incredulous glance through the window, but of course she couldn't see the entrance to the apartment block from there.

Sheer panic hollowed out her stomach. How many times had she rehearsed this scene in the past few days? Yet she was still far from ready. 'You could have used the intercom,' she said inanely.

'Let me in, Jacoba.'

She did, and waited tensely for the bell, wishing that she wore something more chic than jeans and a lambswool jersey. Even if she had her hair pinned up to give her some formality—but it flowed loosely down her back. Not that it mattered— nothing mattered, because she was going to send him away.

When the bell chimed she pinned a smile to her cold lips and forced herself across to open the door.

His splendid vitality seemed dimmed, as though he'd endured the same sleepless nights she had, and he looked at her with eyes that were burnished and opaque. But he couldn't hide the hunger that darkened them, or the fierce smile that curled his beautiful mouth.

If she'd had time to prepare herself—but his unexpected arrival had taken her by storm, and she was fighting a rear-guard action against memories...

Without preamble he said, 'You didn't deserve to be insulted. Forgive me, but I thought that perhaps I had mis-understood and that you were like so many women I meet, eager for payment of some kind.'

'And now you don't?'

'I didn't even then,' he admitted harshly. 'I was disgusted by the journalist who lost no chance to denigrate you when you rejected him, but when you did the same to me I behaved just as badly as he did.' He paused, and when she didn't say anything he went on with curt frankness, 'It was wounded pride. I have a bad temper, though I don't lose it often. I'm very sorry I did with you.'

Dimly, Jacoba realised he hadn't mentioned anything about any connection she might have had with Illyria, so he couldn't have read Border's attempt at revenge. She swallowed to clear her throat before she could say, 'I lost my temper with you too.'

'But you didn't hurl insults you knew were untrue and unfair. I have no right to ask for forgiveness, but I can promise you it will never happen again.'

'It's all right,' she said, her voice small and husky, her mind whirling. 'I shouldn't have let things go so far.'

Abruptly he said, 'You have a perfect right to refuse whenever you want to.' And then his voice changed. 'I won't harass you any more.'

He held out his hand. Don't touch! some instinctual warning shrieked inside her, but it was too late; she'd already automatically put her hand in his. 'You didn't harass me,' she said before she had time to think.

His fingers closed gently around hers. Her skin tightened and she almost flinched at the electric charge of power through her. Without volition she lifted her eyes. What she saw in his made her heart jump.

'I've missed you,' he said roughly.

'I've missed you too,' she whispered.

She had no idea who moved first, but before she could take another breath she was in his arms.

Her resistance stayed in her brain, betrayed by her treacherous body, alive and hot and eager and revived by his touch. Instinctively seeking the solace of his kiss, she lifted her face.

When his mouth took hers she gave a noiseless sigh and abandoned herself to the glory of his presence and his touch.

Incandescent arousal revived every cell in her body so that it clamoured for the fulfilment only he could give her.

Still kissing her, he carried her into the sitting room. Afire with the security of his strength, the heat of his big, lithe body, the barely discernible scent that was his personal signature, she surrendered.

Ever since he left she'd been starving for him, she realised exultantly, and now he was here, and suddenly everything was so simple...

CHAPTER EIGHT

EVERY reason Jacoba had for not wanting this was lost in the haze of delicious, reckless desire that swamped her.

Dimly she realised she had her arms around Marco's neck, was pressed against his lean, very aroused body. Mouth still possessing hers, he set her on her feet. Starved, eager, they kissed until both needed to breathe again. He lifted his head and looked at her with eyes of fire and ice, the magnificent bone structure of his face stark and forceful.

'And I want you,' he said.

The stripped, potent statement was claim, challenge and a statement of intent all at the same time. It fed her desire like tinder on a flame.

Helplessly Jacoba slid her hands up his throat, one palm covering the pulse beating at its base. Grey eyes stormy and intent, she let her fingers slip into his crisp, fine hair.

Every muscle in his big body tightened. He stared at her as though refusing to cede some sort of power. His mouth compressed, and she thought for a moment that he was going to break her hold, but although she could feel the tension radiating from his big body, he still didn't move. Frozen as a predator watching prey, he let her caress him without giving her any reaction.

Responding ardently to the driving thud of his heart beneath her touch, she tempered her unspoken surrender with her own claim. 'I want you.'

His gaze narrowed, lancing into her with the precision of a scalpel. 'Good,' he said, and as though the mere act of talking snapped his ferocious self-discipline, he kissed her again, and this time there was no hesitation from her, no holding back from either of them.

After his searing scrutiny Jacoba expected a wild possession—eagerly anticipated it, in fact, because then she wouldn't have to consider the implications of this total surrender.

But he reimposed control, although the dark blood that emphasised his cheekbones showed how difficult it was. 'Are you sure?'

'Yes,' she said feverishly. She'd never felt like this before—his previous caresses had been a dream of sensuality, but like a dream they'd whetted rather than appeased her hunger for him.

His eyes gleamed. 'I do like a woman who knows her own mind,' he said gravely, before scooping her up in his arms again. 'Direct me.'

Once in her room, Jacoba shivered again, and he said instantly, 'Tell me how to turn up the heat.'

'I'm not cold.' Her voice sounded husky and intimate, and she didn't care what her tone and her words told him.

After another hooded, searching scrutiny he gave the hard, triumphant smile of a lover. 'If you were, I'd warm you,' he promised. 'Raise your arms.'

Obediently, pulses thundering an uneven tattoo through her singing body, she obeyed. Marco slid her jersey over her head, dropping it to run his hands back down her arms in a slow, lingering caress, his eyes darkening as he took in her wide gaze and trembling mouth.

'You are so beautiful,' he said harshly, stroking the curve of one high breast.

Sensation, pure and brilliant as a golden arrow, shot to the smouldering core of her body. Beneath his caressing hands, the centres of both breasts peaked, fiercely expectant.

Marco's smile became fixed; his chest lifted as he dragged in a harsh breath and the crystalline clarity of his gaze intensified into the blue flame at the heart of a diamond. A harsh sound in his throat sent a savage thrill through her.

While he undid the fastening of her bra she unbuttoned his shirt, spreading it so that she could gaze her fill on the broad expanse of bronze chest. Shuddering when his warm hands cupped her supple breasts, she traced the scrolls of hair from one powerful shoulder to the other, then down over the taut sheath of muscle towards his waistline.

The friction against her fingertips was exquisite; emboldened by her freedom to explore, she bent and kissed one hard little nipple, then delicately licked it.

He swore an oath in Illyrian, the words rapid and broken.

The muscles in his shoulders and arms bulged and he lifted her so that her breasts were on a level with his face and took the centre of one in his mouth. Gently at first, then more strongly when soft moans of pleasure burst from her lips, he tasted her.

Tormented by violent need, she pressed herself against his lean strength. He broke off the embrace and lowered her to the bed, standing beside it like some dark conqueror as his eyes feasted on her slender, creamy nakedness.

'You look like some goddess from the sea,' he said, and tore off his trousers and came down beside her. 'When I saw you at the beach, I thought of Venus, rising from the ocean...'

She made a startled movement as he shackled both her hands in one of his and stretched them above her head, anchoring them on the pillows.

'I need to—I want to get undressed,' she protested desperately, wriggling to free herself.

'If you do, it will be all over,' he said roughly. He rested his forehead against hers and went on, 'I used to think that making love with the light off was like making love in a raincoat, but I can see the point of it now. Just looking at you makes me so close to coming I can barely control myself.'

She said between her teeth, 'I'm not going to make love to you like this!'

'Ah, but I can satisfy you,' he said, and slid his free hand beneath her jeans, pushing down the zip.

'Let me go!'

'If you promise not to touch me.'

'Don't be an idiot!' she ground out.

He flung back his head and laughed. 'Very well then, so be it!' he said, and let her go.

Jacoba grabbed both his arms just below the shoulder, her fingers digging into the flexed muscles. He was hot—so hot his skin burned against her palms.

'Marco, if I don't get there with you in me, you can pleasure me afterwards,' she panted.

Like opponents staking out ground, they stared into each other's eyes.

In the end he smiled—a tight, brief movement of his beautiful mouth. 'I think that's only the fourth time you've actually said my name. I like to hear it on your lips. I want to hear it often...'

As he spoke the last word he found her hidden source of pleasure. Overwhelmed, she arched into his hand, still clinging when he brought her to such rapture that she groaned into his mouth and convulsed, hips churning until the final wave of glittering sensation ebbed, leaving her dreamy and replete.

'Now see how long I last,' he said, flicking her jeans from her lax body.

In one strong thrust he entered her. Energised by a resurgence of need, Jacoba gasped and welcomed him in.

She expected him to push further, but for long seconds he lay still, every muscle bunched and taut, as though accustoming himself to her. Opening her eyes, she met his, and that fierce raptor's gaze summoned a response that matched his.

She whispered his name on a slow, yearning note, and muscles she hadn't even known she possessed clamped tightly to hold him inside her, demanding more, claiming his complete surrender.

Marco frowned, as though he read the snatches of thought racing through her brain, then deliberately, he withdrew. Before she had time to protest, he thrust again, the muscles in his powerful shoulders bunching beneath his sleek bronze skin.

This time she called out, a broken little sound ripped from her heart, and he smiled and repeated the slow, tantalising withdrawal, the controlled entry, setting up a rhythm as tormenting as it was addictive.

More adrenalin rushed through Jacoba, sharpening her senses to almost painful stimulation. Her lashes drifted down; intoxicated by reckless desire, she surrendered to the heady, exhilarating tension that slowly built in every cell of her body, forcing her further and further towards another release.

It came violently, like lightning, like thunder—wave after wave of passionate striving that lifted her high into another plane of existence. Their bodies were so in tune that as she reached her greatest ecstasy he came with her, his thick, impeded groan echoing in the charged silence of the room.

Every muscle in the big body flexed and his arms around her tightened; together they climbed one final peak and soared into mind-shattering fulfilment.

And came down lazily, sweetly, locked in each other's arms, the only sound in the room their harsh breathing and the mingled thudding of their two hearts.

Eventually his arms loosened. When she clung for a desperate moment, he kissed her temple and said tenderly, 'Dear heart, I'll turn over—I'm too heavy.'

Jacoba whispered, 'No, you're not,' but he turned on his side anyway, manoeuvring her to lie half on top of him. Drained and at peace, she felt her body purr at the contact. In a way, she thought dimly, sleep shadowing the fringes of her mind, this was even sweeter than making love.

Like this, cherished and surrounded by the scent and feel of him, she could fool herself for a few seconds into thinking that Marco felt more for her than simple lust…

Much later, when they'd loved again, and again, one strong hand pushed her hair back from her face, the damp strands clinging to his fingers. He said, 'You have hair like fire.'

'It was the scourge of my childhood,' she murmured, pressing her face into the hollow between his throat and the arrogant jut of his jaw so that the words were kisses against his skin.

They lay in silence and eventually her eyes closed and she let unconsciousness take over.

When she woke it was high morning, and she was alone in her big bed. She lay still, listening, but she could feel the emptiness in the apartment.

Marco had gone. Oh, he'd told her while they lay in each other's arms that he was due at a meeting in Dubai the next day, but his absence stung—no, it *hurt*, a raw, painful ache in some secret part of her that had never been touched before.

Blinking back hot, stupid tears, she forced herself to relax. After all, he'd made no promises, and neither had she; probably all he wanted was a quick, short-lived affair to get her out of his system, then a farewell with no bones broken, no hearts shattered. He'd certainly made sure there would be no chance of pregnancy.

That was what she wanted too. Anything else was too dangerous.

She should steel herself to get up, but memories drifted into her mind, seducing her with their sweetness, their passion...

They'd made love like enemies, and then like lovers, and when it was over she'd lain in his arms and known herself to be safe...

He'd called her 'Dear heart,' an old Illyrian endearment...

She could still hear the syllables, his voice deep and quiet, as though it was the first time he'd ever used the love-words.

Jacoba stiffened and her eyes opened wide. He'd spoken in Illyrian. And she'd answered. Feverishly she searched through her memory, replaying the conversation again in her mind.

Yes, he'd spoken in Illyrian—and although some unregenerate part of her rejoiced that he'd been so blown away by the experience that he'd used his native language, she shivered.

'Dear heart, I'll turn over—I'm too heavy.'

And then, much later, *'You have hair like fire.'*

Had she answered in the same language? Try as she would, she couldn't pull her words from the recesses of her brain.

She thought she might have used English for her first answer, but she had a horrifying suspicion that her second had been in Illyrian.

Not that it mattered what she'd spoken—her answer had betrayed her, because it made it plain that she understood his native language.

Oh, you *idiot!* she castigated herself, panic hitting hard and fast like a kick in the stomach. Like so many foolish people down the centuries, she'd allowed sated passion to loosen her control so that she'd succumbed to the perils of pillow talk.

Because although Marco's cold, incisive mind might have

been hazed by the aftermath of passion, it wouldn't stay that way. Even if he hadn't noticed last night, he'd remember sooner or later that she understood Illyrian.

And then he'd wonder why she hadn't told him about it.

Wondering would lead to action and, with all the power and resources at his command, that would inevitably bring to light Gregory Border's comments in his column about connections to Illyria.

Adrenalin rode her hard. Once more she tried to convince herself that with the dreaded cadres of Illyrian secret police disbanded years previously, neither she nor Lexie had anything to fear.

But she'd have to warn her sister that the safe haven their mother had struggled to create had been breached.

Jacoba glanced at her watch. It would be evening in Australia; if Lexie had her mobile phone turned on—and if there was coverage in the Outback, which she doubted—she might be able to contact her.

After dialling she waited impatiently, her tension increasing until she was forced to accept that Lexie wasn't going to answer. Biting her lip, she fired up her laptop and dashed off an email, hoping that somewhere in the red deserts of central Australia her sister might be able to access a computer.

If only she hadn't succumbed to the urge to tell Marco that she and Hawke weren't lovers! Now she'd have to convince him that last night was a one-off, an experience that would never be repeated.

He'd despise her. The knowledge hurt, keen as a dagger to her heart.

It was all over the most energetic of the tabloids the next evening. 'Prince Marco's New Lover,' screamed the headlines, accompanied by grainy photographs.

'Oh, no,' she moaned, pushing a trembling hand through her hair. This was all she needed!

Feeling as though everyone's eyes were on her, she bought a copy and raced home to read the piece with outrage that turned rapidly to fear.

The columnist in Auckland had sold his information to London, and the connection to Illyria was hinted at again. She tried to feel grateful that Lexie wasn't mentioned.

Some malicious creature had selected a picture of her in the most outrageous outfit she'd ever modelled, an avant-garde evening dress on the catwalk at the Paris collections years before. It had made great play with her long legs and her breasts; she hadn't enjoyed wearing it, and it made her cringe now.

'The prince and the tart,' she muttered, looking at the one of Marco, lean and powerful in ski clothes, snapped at the bottom of a piste in Switzerland.

Fortunately she was booked for three days in the Cayman Islands; she was ambushed by photographers when she left, but she smiled and ignored them. And while posing in the tropical sun she was free of the Press, but the mental freedom she so longed for was harder to achieve.

Because Prince Marco Considine seemed to have taken up permanent residence in her life. Three of the four magazines in her airy hotel room had articles about him—all with photographs.

Of course, those chiselled Mediterranean features, all angles and aristocratic bones, photographed brilliantly.

'You should have been a model,' she said sourly to one snapshot. 'You'd have made a fortune!'

The night before she was due back in London, she finally got an email from Lexie. It began with a bombshell.

Mama was terrified of the secret police because she was the dictator's wife. He was my father.

Stunned, her heart jumping wildly in her chest, Jacoba stared at the bleak words. 'No!' she muttered.

With incredulous eyes, she read the rest of her sister's letter.

Blood feuds are a way of life in Illyria, especially in the mountains, which is where Mama and the Considines come from. Prince Alex is trying to stamp them out, but they still happen. If anyone can prove who you are, you'll be in real danger. I'll be OK—very few people know I'm your sister.

It finished with her signature, but beneath she'd written,

I'll understand if you don't want anything to do with me. Mama said that PC had your father killed so he could marry her. She was forced to because he threatened to kill you.

'Oh, God,' Jacoba breathed, gripped by appalled nausea.

She wasn't the one in danger. If blood feuds were still a factor in Illyrian society Lexie would be the target once anyone found out that she was Paulo Considine's daughter.

Jacoba didn't dare discount the whole horrifying, mediaeval idea. Lexie was methodical and practical; she'd have done the research. If she said blood feuds were a problem in Illyria, they were.

After failing to get through on the phone to Lexie, she dashed off an answer, indignantly asserting that she loved her sister and not to be such an idiot, and for heaven's sake, stay in the Outback until they'd worked out what to do…

She spent the next few hours researching on the internet. It was definitely true, so she then tried to come up with plans to protect her sister. In the end the only thing that made sense was to let Marco know.

But what if he believed in blood feuds? No, she thought, surely he didn't. She got to her feet and strode across to the window, staring sightlessly out. Her turmoil eased.

She'd accept that he was ruthless, but she couldn't conceive the sophisticated man she knew indulging in something as primitive and violent as a feud to the death.

Besides, he'd been born and grown up in France, that most civilised of countries. If anyone would know how to deal with this situation, it was Marco, and for Lexie's sake she'd ask. Mind whirling, she switched on the television. And there, smiling aloofly, was the prince.

'You're haunting me!' she muttered, unwillingly sinking into a chair.

She spent the next half-hour listening and watching. He handled the interview brilliantly, like the pro he was, his natural charm and authority and intelligence almost outdoing his physical splendour.

Her heart clenched; why, of all the men in the world, did she have to want this forbidden one?

She'd only been back in London a day when her telephone rang. 'It's Marco Considine,' he said. 'Let me in.'

Pulse racing, she activated the lock and stood tensely, waiting for him to come through the door. The moment she saw him she knew he was angry. Even though it was fiercely controlled, it emanated from him like an ice-cold aura.

He knows, she thought, apprehension flooding her. *He knows...*

Shivering, she said, 'What is it? Why are you here?'

'What do you have to tell me?' Marco's English was faultless, the accent impeccable, but beneath it she heard the same intonation that had underlined her mother's English.

Unable to think, she stalled, falling back a step or two to say, 'I don't know what you mean.'

'I'm sure you do,' he said contemptuously, and held out an envelope. 'Read this.'

Nervously she took out the document inside and glanced at it. The first words drove the colour from her face; she groped for the back of the chair with one hand and clung, her eyes searching the page.

Oh, how Gregory Border must have laughed when Marco warned him off. Well, he'd got his revenge. How long had he known who she and Lexie were? She read further, colour storming into her face as the story unfolded.

When she'd finished she lifted her head and said furiously, 'This—this is a farrago of lies! How *dare* he?'

In a voice totally devoid of intonation and warmth, he said, 'It is the truth. As you must know.'

She didn't even realise he was speaking in Illyrian. She said fiercely, 'My father was not Illyrian—he was a Scotsman who died fighting Paulo Considine's forces in the mountains.'

'He certainly died in the ambush that killed my grandparents, but he was an Illyrian doctor,' he stated with cold precision. 'And your sister is the daughter of Paulo Considine.'

A huge fist of pain clenched inside her chest, and she turned her face away hastily in case he saw it reflected in her eyes. 'I know that. But the rest is total lies.'

His lip curled. 'What part do you not believe? That your mother was Paulo Considine's mistress and then his wife? What did she tell you?'

Furious, Jacoba cried, 'Nothing—nothing! But I know she wasn't his mistress!'

'I have proof,' he said mercilessly.

The whiplash of disgust in his tone told her all she needed to know. Angrily she demanded, 'What proof?'

'Photographs of them together—not many, but there are some. Photographs of you and your sister—newspaper headlines. It was no secret; he boasted of his lovely wife and his child.'

She shook her head so violently that the room whirled. 'No,' she said again, but this time more quietly. Her huge, desperate eyes searched his, and she read the hard truth in their chilling depths.

'I think perhaps your mother didn't want her children to understand the situation,' he said courteously. 'Perfectly natural on her part.'

'You're so wrong.' But her voice faltered and she rubbed a shaking hand over her mouth.

He watched her keenly, his handsome face hard and remote as some granite monolith. 'It is not your sister's fault that she was born to the wrong parents. Nor yours,' he added with scrupulous fairness. 'I have already set things in motion to dampen any media interest.'

Stung into indiscretion, she retorted angrily, 'I don't believe my mother was his mistress—or if she was, it was under duress. She hated Paulo Considine! She was terrified of him.'

'She may have been, but she betrayed her first husband—your father, and the partisans—to him.' Marco was implacable, his handsome face stern and judicial.

'She did not,' she said between her teeth, hands clenching at her sides as she stared at him, sudden fear crumbling her composure. Surely he wasn't bound by the strictures of the blood feud?

Dry-mouthed, she went on desperately, 'She would never have betrayed anyone—she was the most honest, upright, loyal person I've ever met.'

'Even honest, upright, loyal people can be manipulated,' he said, his steely tone not giving an inch. 'Did she not tell you anything about her life in Illyria?'

'She rarely spoke of it,' she admitted, adding when she saw his eyes narrow, 'and she was terrified the secret police would find her.'

Marco's abrupt gesture signified a complete lack of interest. 'Whether you believe me or not makes no difference. Your sister is a Considine,' he said with icy, unsparing clarity. 'You are both the daughter of a woman who betrayed about fifteen people to the dictator's forces. They all died—some cut down by bullets, some at his hands, some at those of his torturers.'

Shattered, she stared at him. 'As soon as my mother was able to, she took us and fled. Doesn't that tell you anything?'

'It tells me that even the most power-hungry women can sometimes be good mothers.' He held up a hand to stop her instant objection. 'And that she was clever enough to see that since she was no longer able to give him a son—'

'What do you mean?'

Straight black brows rose. 'There were such problems at the birth of your sister that your mother could have no other children. The dictator wanted a son. At the very least he would have divorced her; most probably she saw a drastically cur- tailed future for both herself and her children. So she ran.'

'I don't believe you,' she repeated numbly, unable to recon- cile her gentle mother with this bloodstained drama of the past.

'Your loyalty does you credit,' Marco returned with that chilling courtesy. 'But none of this is particularly important. I want you to ring your sister and tell her to prepare for a journey to Illyria.'

Suddenly afraid, Jacoba asked harshly, 'Why?'

'Because it is possible there are Illyrian refugees in New

Zealand or Australia who still harbour a grudge,' he admitted. He paused, then went on, 'Did your mother speak of the blood feuds in Illyria, especially among the mountain people?'

'I— Yes,' she whispered, cold fear scrambling her brain. 'But not a lot.'

'That is what she was afraid of,' he said. 'The secret police, yes, but also that relatives of one of the people she betrayed— possibly your father, who was much loved—would hunt her down and kill her.'

'And us?' The words sounded stilted.

He shrugged. 'It is possible,' he said.

Terrified now for Lexie's sake, she shook her head again. 'Do they—the Illyrians—really believe that my mother betrayed all those people?' She scanned his handsome, ruthless face with something close to horror, her wide eyes alert to anything that might indicate he was lying.

'It was no secret,' he said bluntly. 'Paulo Considine made sure everyone knew—probably his way of being certain she had no allies. So there is a possibility that someone might seek revenge. That is the last thing I want.'

She shook her head. Inside she felt dead, but stubborn will-power drove her to say, 'It's nothing to do with you.'

'It is everything to do with me.' Jacoba shook her head, but he continued, 'If Illyria is going to become a modern country the hunger for personal revenge must be wiped from the national consciousness. So we—all Illyrians— must learn to forgive. Also, your sister is a Considine, and we protect our own.'

Impersonal, without warmth, his scrutiny hurt. She pressed the back of her hand to her dry lips, then let it fall limply to her side. Tonelessly she said, 'I don't know whether I can trust you. If what you say is true, then you and your brother—and Prince Alex—are the ones who are most likely to want to kill Lexie.'

'And you,' he said ruthlessly. 'You are not safe either. You inherit the burden of your mother's treachery.'

She flinched, and he went on, 'Blood feuds are a response to a society where justice is rare and flawed. They have no place in the modern world. Part of Alex's task—and that of all of us who escaped the dictator's cruelty—is to convince the people of the mountains that they can safely leave justice to the state.' He lifted her chin, forcing her to meet his eyes. 'Do you believe that you and your sister are safe from any sort of revenge attempt by us?'

Words trembled on her lips, silenced by the intensity of his piercing regard. This man had taken her to paradise in his arms, but she didn't know him well enough to be sure. Then she thought of his reputation in business—ruthless but fair—and his gentleness when they'd made love, his concern for her pleasure, his tenderness afterwards.

She swallowed and whispered, 'Yes. I do.'

He nodded. 'Once the Illyrians see that we Considines have accepted you, any fuss will die down and you and your sister will be safe.'

The assured, uncompromising words hit her like stones. She stared at his formidable face, searching for some sign of the warmth they'd shared. There was nothing. He was watching her with a cold detachment that tore her heart to shreds.

In the end she turned away. 'Is that the only way to deal with it?' she said thinly.

'I believe so. Our relationship has been noted, so it is a simple step to becoming engaged.'

'*What?*'

Stunned, his deliberate words dancing crazily around her head, she stared at him. His transparent eyes were icily commanding, and his mouth set in lines that told her he wasn't joking. He looked perfectly sane, as much master of this situation as he was of all others, while everything was careering out of her control.

'No,' she said, her heart a heavy lump in her chest. 'That's a crazy idea.'

'It may save the sister you profess to love from a degree of unpleasantness,' he told her bluntly. 'Or worse.'

'I—' Mind scurrying for objections, she stared at his unyielding face. In the end she whispered, 'Are you sure?'

'Do you think I *want* this?' he asked with cold scorn.

She flushed. 'No.'

'Becoming engaged to me will signal that as a family, we Considines don't intend to pursue any feud.'

'But how is that going to protect us if someone else decides to satisfy their desire for revenge? I can't prove my mother didn't betray the partisan group.' She looked into his stern, autocratic face with rising desperation. 'Nobody can, not now.'

Marco shrugged negligently. 'As the family commonly supposed to have suffered the most, our right to pursue a feud is paramount. Once we make it clear that we don't want any more deaths, any more killing, it will finish.'

'Can you be sure of that?'

He nodded. 'The custom was barbaric, but it had rules and regulations. I am not lying, Jacoba—this is too important for lies.'

She hesitated, unsure of whether to trust him or not.

His mouth sketched a sardonic smile. 'And even when feuds were a part of life, there was a well-known way of ending them.'

Some note in his voice whipped her head around. 'Which was?'

'Marrying a daughter of the house to one of the antagonists often sealed the peace.' His smile was tight and humourless, his eyes guarded and watchful.

CHAPTER NINE

'MARRIAGE?' Jacoba's heart leapt, and then sank as she searched Marco's inflexible features. Of course he didn't mean it.

And she wouldn't marry him even if he did. Because, she realised bleakly, somewhere, somehow—she didn't even know when or why—she'd fallen in love with him. He'd taken over her life in a thousand subtle ways, and while she'd been trying to convince herself that she was only physically attracted to him, her heart had slipped from her keeping and found another home.

Sure enough, he said decisively, 'We will not need to take it so far. An engagement will be enough. Eventually, when emotions have died down enough to make you and your sister safe, we can end it amicably.'

'But…' Jacoba paused, her heart shredding inside her. 'What about your brother?'

'What about him?' Marco demanded, black brows drawing together.

'He'll hate Lexie too—and me, if he thinks my mother betrayed your grandparents.' No longer able to contain it, she heard her hurt pour out in a torrent. She dragged in a sharp breath, achieving enough control to be able to finish, 'And how will Prince Alex react?'

'I have discussed it with both Gabe and Alex,' he said curtly, 'and they agree that this is the best way to tackle a very difficult situation.'

'But it might not be necessary.' The very idea of blood feuds was outrageous in this gracious room, so civilised and sophisticated in the English way. She pushed a shaking hand through her hair and tried desperately to convince him. 'You don't *know* that some Illyrian filled with fantasies of a blood feud is going to lose his head and come gunning for Lexie.'

'And I don't know that one won't,' he returned implacably. 'That is the stark truth. You find it hard to believe because such things don't happen in your nice, safe New Zealand.'

'It has villains too,' she said miserably. She cast another anguished glance at his implacable expression, and felt the steel jaws of a trap closing around her. Everything he said made sense.

'But in New Zealand the villains don't subscribe to outdated ideas of honour and revenge,' Marco said unsparingly. 'For many years the Illyrians have had nothing but their own indomitable spirit and the stories of the heroes of their past to sustain them, and part of that history was the blood feud. If we do not do this, I cannot guarantee your safety.'

'That's not your responsibility,' she said bleakly.

'My brother and I are agreed that it is.'

He scanned her downcast face, an odd sensation gripping him. There was much to admire in her loyalty to both her dead mother and her sister. He found himself wondering if she was as loyal to her lovers.

Making up his mind, he said harshly, 'Only a year ago a man was killed in a suspected blood feud. Prince Alex stated that the perpetrator would be hunted down and face a trial for his actions.'

The colour left her skin. 'Was he caught?'

'Yes. And tried. He admitted it, but the jury acquitted him.'

'*Acquitted* him?' She stared at him, her eyes huge. Hands knotting in front of her, she said quietly, 'So it's deeply in-grained in the national psyche.'

He'd known her quick mind would catch the implications. 'Exactly. Because Alex is trying to introduce the rule of law he was forced to release him, but after conferring with the council and parliament, he decided that in future he, with the aid of two senior judges, will try anyone else accused of a revenge killing. But as yet no one knows if this will be enough to stop them.'

His words wore Jacoba down. She looked down at her fingers, held still by will-power. For the first time in her life she wanted to fling herself onto the floor and scream and have hysterics—utterly impossible in the face of his iron composure. 'Tell me truly—if I say no, do you think Lexie will be in danger?'

His answer came instantly. 'I believe it is possible you are both in danger. So do my brother and the trusted men Prince Alex has consulted.'

Jacoba's heart sank as she read the truth in his uncompromising expression and the tough line of his mouth. Briefly she closed her eyes.

He went on calmly, 'And if you refuse I will have both you and your sister transferred to Gabe's castle in Illyria, where you'll stay until I decide that it's safe for you to resume your ordinary lives.'

He meant it. Jacoba's heart lurched. 'You're an arrogant bastard,' she flared.

'But you know I will do it.'

'Yes,' she admitted wearily. 'And I'm sure that you wouldn't be going so far if you didn't really believe what you're saying.' Eyes aching with unshed tears, she finished,

'But I want you to promise that you're prepared—at the very least—to accept the possibility that my mother was incapable of betraying anyone. You didn't know her; I did. She couldn't have done it.'

He shrugged, his gaze very cold and blue. 'I have already said that I don't believe the sins of the fathers should be visited on their children. I know she was a good mother, that she worked long hours and sacrificed everything for you when you were young. The rest is not important.'

'It is to me,' she said, not giving an inch.

His icy scrutiny didn't spare her. Tension flashed between them, swift and strong as lightning. After a few moments he said shortly, 'Very well. As it is so important to you, I accept your terms.'

'Hardly a gracious concession,' she snapped.

And knew she should have kept quiet. But he said remotely, 'I know this is difficult, but I believe that at the moment it is necessary.'

Abruptly surrendering, Jacoba nodded. 'Too many lives have already been squandered in Illyria to risk any more bloodshed.'

'I'm glad you see it that way.'

'So what happens now?' she asked tautly, apprehension hollowing her stomach.

'Our engagement will be announced tomorrow. Where is your sister?'

'Why do you want to know?'

'I want her in Illyria, where we can protect her.'

When she hesitated, he said crisply, 'Make up your mind, Jacoba. Either you trust me, or you don't. Now that this journalist has revealed who you are, we may not have time to waste. There are Illyrian refugees in New Zealand.'

He knew the right buttons to press. And she did trust him—

the formidable pride she'd seen in him convinced her that he wouldn't take revenge on an innocent victim of the dictator's cruelty. But it took every ounce of courage and faith she possessed to reveal Lexie's whereabouts. If she was wrong…

In the end she had to. At some deeper level she trusted him to do whatever he could to protect her sister.

He said, 'I'll put someone on to it straight away. Can you warn her what to expect? It will be less alarming for her if she knows what's happening.'

His thoughtfulness should have warmed her, but she could only think that if he did intend them any harm, a complaisant Lexie would make things easier. 'Internet cafés aren't common in the Outback.'

'The agency that organised the tour must have some way to contact them,' he said crisply. 'Don't worry. I'll make sure she gets safely away.' He glanced at his watch. 'A jeweller should be arriving any minute with a choice of rings for you— I suggest a ruby. As well as being the traditional stone of my house, the colour suits you.'

In a flat voice she said, 'You had no doubt that you could browbeat me into this, did you?'

He measured her with an unwavering look. 'I owe the people of Illyria my duty—and so do you. If you are not of Paulo Considine's get you are the daughter of a doctor who died in a hail of bullets with my grandparents, and whose family were killed too. You owe *their* memories respect, as well as your mother's.'

Trust him to turn her stipulation against her! 'That's not fair,' she choked.

'Fairness—what is that? This is a matter of justice.' A humourless smile didn't soften his mouth. 'And before you ask, you need have no fears that I will expect you to be my mistress while we're engaged. That is over.'

The detached, decisive words were like hammer blows to her heart. His mistress? Well, she'd always known that he wanted nothing more than sex from her.

Pride as stiff and unbending as his drove her to say, 'After I'd told you what I knew of our history, I was going to make sure you understood that.'

'Then we are in accord,' he said cynically, and turned as the manservant appeared in the doorway. 'This must be the jeweller.'

The only way to get through this was to tamp down her feelings and go on to automatic pilot, calling on the acting skills she'd achieved over the years to fake it. So tense that she felt she might shatter any moment, Jacoba summoned spurious interest to examine the array of rings brought for her selection.

'Try that one,' Marco said, his voice tender as he pointed at a ruby that glowed with dark fire. Set around the stone were gems in a soft gold that enhanced and contrasted with the ruby. The ring should have looked flashy, but the skill of its creator and the juxtaposition of colours gave it a dramatic, exotic splendour.

'It is not conventional,' the jeweller said when Jacoba hesitated. 'Perhaps *madame* would prefer a solitaire.' He glanced at her hands, tensely clasped at her sides. 'She has the fingers for it,' he said, and indicated a massive diamond.

'Too flashy,' she said indifferently. Her gaze slid back to the first ring. It didn't look like an engagement ring…

'That one,' she said, making up her mind.

It fitted perfectly—but then, Marco probably had all her measurements filed away in his incisive brain, she thought painfully. He knew them well enough—his lean, skilful hands had caressed every inch of her body.

Light shimmered and glittered in the heart of the main stone. 'Perfect,' Marco said austerely.

Once they were alone Jacoba said, 'What happens now?'

'We leave for Illyria in an hour.'

When she flashed him a startled glance and started to shake her head, he took her elbow and turned her to face him. His tone dispassionate, he said, 'I know you have no bookings until the ball next week to launch the perfume. Get used to this farce we're playing, Jacoba. If it helps, think of your part in it as paying back a little of the damage your step-father caused.'

'How?' she asked truculently, twisting free.

He switched to Illyrian. 'It might bring about a change in attitude that will ultimately benefit all Illyrians. Although it's less tangible than the money you have regularly sent to Illyrian charities ever since Alex came to the throne, it is perhaps more important in the long run.'

Heat flooded Jacoba's skin. In the same language, she asked impetuously, 'How did you know—?' stopping when she saw his cynical smile. 'I sent that money anonymously.'

'It wasn't too difficult to discover who was sending such large sums.'

Not difficult at all if you had the money and the power to set a firm of private detectives on the hunt, she thought bleakly.

He went on, 'It's been very welcome, but you owe a tribute of blood also.'

The oddly antique words sent a shiver down her spine. 'An eye for an eye?'

Marco frowned. 'Nothing so vengeful.' His gaze dropped to her mouth. In exactly the same tone he said, 'And if you want to make sure your sister is safe, you'll give everyone we meet the idea that you are deeply, devotedly in love with me. As I will with you.'

The cynical words twisted her heart. 'No doubt my acting skills will come in handy.'

'I am sure of it,' he said courteously. Reverting to English, he went on, 'You're looking pale. This whole business has been a shock to you. The housekeeper at the castle will be in her element. She is very fond of cosseting people.'

The sun glowed golden on the white tops of the mountains as the helicopter came down to land near a castle that looked like something out of a fairy tale—a dark fairy tale, Jacoba thought with a twist of her heart.

Beside her, Marco said, 'The Wolf's Lair. Unfortunately, Gabe isn't here—he sends his apologies, but he is in the capital at the moment.'

A thin surge of cowardly panic battled with excitement.

Here in the valley where it had all happened, an uneasy apprehension kept her tense and jumpy; she felt as though someone—or some*thing*—had been waiting a long time for her to arrive.

After dinner that night, Marco inspected her with hooded eyes. 'You're tired,' he said.

Tired and heartsick. 'It's been a long day.'

'So go to bed.'

Marco escorted her to her room, pushing open the door for her. She was about to step past him when he turned her into his arms and kissed her with a pent-up hunger that set her on fire. She clung to his strength, wondering if this flash-fire of passion could possibly be enough...

And then he released her, and she realised that an elderly woman was moving silently about in the room.

Sickened, she realised why he'd kissed her.

'You met Marya this afternoon,' Marco said smoothly. 'She has worked for us all her life, and is now the housekeeper in the castle.'

Jacoba smiled at her, and gave the traditional Illyrian greeting. 'May God bless you and all your children.'

The housekeeper smiled back, her dark eyes intent and measuring. 'And yours. And may your sleep be free of dreams.'

She nodded almost regally and took herself off down the stone-floored passage, past portraits of long-dead Considines and several stunning landscapes. A suit of armour stood guard at the end beside a bookcase.

It couldn't have been more different from everything she'd known, Jacoba thought on a wave of homesickness for New Zealand. Ignoring it, she said quietly, 'She has a powerful personality.'

'Yes.' Marco paused, then said, 'As a family we are beholden to her.'

Jacoba looked up sharply. Angular face unreadable, he went on, 'She hid the Queen's Blood from the dictator, and suffered because of her loyalty.'

Jacoba nodded; she'd heard of the Queen's Blood, the ancient treasure of the family—a set of rubies in gold that was infinitely valuable and so old no one knew who'd made it or when.

Marco said, 'Tomorrow morning we'll go riding, so sleep well.'

She didn't, until she took one of the mild sleeping pills she used occasionally to settle into a new time zone. And even then her rest was uneasy and punctuated by snatches of nightmare, and she woke early, lying for an hour or so with slow tears aching behind her eyes.

Giving in to them wasn't going to achieve anything but red eyes, so she forced herself out of bed, showered and got into jeans and a black merino jersey.

A knock at her door heralded the housekeeper, who carried a tray of coffee and fruit and cheese, and some of the solid, rustic bread her mother had used to bake as a treat now and then.

'To keep you until breakfast,' the older woman said,

putting it on a table near one of the diamond-paned windows. 'Eat now. The prince has been called to the tele-phone.' She sighed, then shrugged. 'All the time, it rings, rings, rings. He sent you a newspaper—from England. And one from here.'

The newspapers made great play of the lost family of the dictator. And whether in fear of Considine power or the skill of the family spin doctors, most of the Press decided to treat the whole thing as hugely romantic, with two different sides of the family being at last reconciled.

There was nothing about Ilona Sinclair being the dictator's mistress, nothing about any suspected betrayal of her husband or Marco's grandparents. Relieved, Jacoba forced down some of the fruit and drank the coffee while the older woman bustled around tidying her room and the small bathroom off it.

Then she escorted Jacoba down to the hall where Marco stood talking to his brother, Gabriele, Grand Duke of Illyria, who'd arrived back late the previous night.

They showed their heritage, Jacoba thought, aching with a fiercely restrained hunger. Through a great window the rays of the rising sun summoned blue flames from two dark heads, and lovingly caressed proud Mediterranean features.

Both men looked up as they came towards them, but Jacoba only had eyes for her prince.

Heat kindled in his pale eyes. 'Jacoba,' he said, and held out his hand to her.

She retained enough poise to manage a swift smile at the Grand Duke as she was introduced, then felt her tension easing a little when Marco tucked her against his lithe body. It was like being born again.

'So where do you plan to go?' Prince Gabe asked, his eyes speculative as he glanced at his brother.

'You should take her to the stone,' the housekeeper interpolated before Marco could answer. She smiled at them all as though she'd arranged such a striking tableau herself.

Gabe looked as though he was about to make a comment, but the words stayed unsaid.

Marco surveyed Jacoba. 'Do you want to see the standing stone?' he asked. 'It's a monolith close to the pass, and occupies a special place in our family history.'

He was, she thought painfully, as good an actor as she was—better, perhaps, because no one could miss the tenderness in his voice and the glitter deep in his eyes.

'In the *country's* history,' Gabe said, his tone giving nothing away.

Jacoba smiled. 'I'd like that. New Zealand has only about a thousand years of history—and there aren't any standing stones.'

The housekeeper said flatly, 'You are Illyrian.'

Marco said, 'By birth and breeding, yes, but I think she'll always be a New Zealander in her heart.'

Surprised at his understanding, Jacoba nodded.

Halfway up the steep, forested slope, she kept her gaze fixed between the ears on her rangy black gelding and observed, 'Your housekeeper seems—very knowing. An old soul.'

'She's had a hard life. Paulo Considine was especially cruel to anyone who had any connection with the family; Marya was a maid at the castle, and she suffered—she lost her family, lost everything except her life.'

Chilled, Jacoba said quietly, 'She doesn't seem to bear me any grudge.'

'Apparently she knew your mother,' he said on a casual note that belied the keen look he gave her.

Her heart jumped. 'Did she?'

'Like you, she doesn't believe that your mother was Paulo's mistress. Or that she betrayed the partisans.'

She sent him a swift, challenging glance. 'I just hope

everyone else in Illyria agrees with her. But that's not going to help Lexie, is it.' It was a statement, not a question.

'She'll be safe,' he said confidently. 'Do you think I'd bring her here if I'd thought we couldn't protect her?'

'I keep wondering…'

She stopped, because she couldn't explain the tension between her shoulder blades, as though someone was watching, planning, waiting for something to happen.

Marco nudged his mount closer. 'Trust me,' he said, and added grimly, 'Or if you can't do that, trust Gabe's security men and Alex's honour.'

Last night, lying in his bed racked with desire for Jacoba, he'd thought again that none of his family had been brought up in Illyria. Although they'd grown up steeped in its history and traditions, only Alex had actually lived there, and then only for the first ten years of his life.

When he'd mooted the idea of an engagement, he and Gabe had consulted Marya, who'd said calmly, 'Of course you must marry her.'

'But will it help?'

She'd shrugged. 'It is the *only* thing that will help.'

He hoped so. God, he hoped so. And not just for the future well-being of the Illyrians, either; if anything happened to Jacoba's sister she'd be shattered.

Jacoba looked at him now, her grey eyes very direct and candid. 'I trust you all. Anyway, what else can we do? Lexie was safe as long as nobody suspected who we were, but as soon as that journalist in Auckland started prying, we were living on borrowed time.'

'He only started looking because I came on the scene,' Marco said grimly.

Vehemently she shook her head. 'Absolutely not! He'd have begun to poke and pry when I turned him down. It was nothing to do with you.' Bitterness tinged her voice. 'You have enough responsibilities without adding another one to your list!'

Marco changed the subject by nodding ahead. 'We've reached the stone. Get down; we'll tie the horses over there.'

Jacoba did as he said, stretching to ease her legs. She felt as though she'd been kicked. Secretly, without even realising, she'd hoped—oh, she'd hoped that perhaps there was something more to this mock-engagement than his sense of duty.

And lust.

Mustn't forget the lust, she thought sarcastically, walking beside him through the trees. She loved him, but Marco felt nothing more than a fierce desire, and even that seemed to be waning. No doubt he resented being forced into an engagement that meant nothing.

A little exclamation of surprise broke from her when they came through the trees into a small, grassy dell.

'It's huge,' she breathed, staring at the massive, upright stone. 'How many men must it have taken to lift it on its end?'

'Hundreds,' he said shortly.

It had been carefully placed; a tiny stream ran through the trees and around its base, then across the grass to disappear into a grove of dark conifers. The silence was broken only by the soft chatter of water as it spilled over a cliff some distance away through the trees.

Awed, Jacoba shivered. 'Tell me I'm crazy, that it doesn't seem to be aware of us,' she muttered.

He said coolly, 'It's supposed to be haunted by the spirit of one of my ancestors, a woman who was murdered here for the treasure she carried—the Queen's Blood.'

Tension prickled across her skin. 'Is that how the treasure came into your family?'

'Not exactly. It's an old story; she was a queen and when bandits killed her here she turned into a sprite—a ghost—and guarded her treasure until the first Considine came here, possibly from Greece. She then manifested herself to him in human form, and eventually he married her. According to the peasants, all Considines are descended from that marriage.'

CHAPTER TEN

FOR a long, charged moment Marco looked at her from beneath heavy lashes, his mouth compressed. Tension tightened Jacoba's nerves and brought her head up in a rapid, defiant gesture.

When he broke the silence it was in a rough, almost desperate voice. 'Don't look at me like that.'

'I don't know what you mean,' Jacoba said, heart thumping crazily.

He came towards her. 'Like an utterly desirable challenge,' he said as his arms closed around her willing body.

And he kissed her, pent-up passion bursting through the iron restraint of his control.

She clung to him, fingers digging into muscles so tense they were like steel, giving Marco so much more than her mouth—letting her kiss say all the things she didn't dare.

For long moments it was enough—the kisses, the muttered words spoken in a mixture of languages, the soaring heat of desire fuelling an even more intense hunger.

And then he let her go. 'I'm sorry,' he said, face and voice so controlled she had to turn away so that he couldn't see the misery in her eyes. 'I made you a promise.'

She'd tied her hair in a pony-tail; she reached up now and

pulled off the tie, letting a lock fall over her face. The movement gave her enough time to force her clamouring body into stillness. 'It's all right,' she said remotely, bolstering her composure with fierce pride.

She sensed rather than saw him move, but as she turned to follow his gaze he swung violently around and pushed her in behind him, clamping her against the stone so that she couldn't move, could barely breathe.

Something like an electric shock ran through her; she gasped and pushed at his big, taut body, frantic to get away. 'What—?' she spluttered, sudden primitive terror rendering her witless. Hideous thoughts of bears and wolves flashed across her mind.

'Quiet,' he growled.

She froze, senses so heightened she heard the soft call of a bird in the trees, the small chirrup of an insect close by, the soft whispering of the tiny stream at her feet, smelt the perfume of crushed grass and pine balsam. And over it, she thought wildly, the subtle alteration to his body scent that indicated an elemental change in him, the subliminal sound of his blood coursing through his body, the hyper-awareness of a man preparing for danger. Pinned out of harm's way, Jacoba regulated her breathing so that she could pick up any slight sound that might indicate an intruder.

For long minutes he stayed still and silent as a predator, until slowly his big body relaxed.

Without moving he said in an undertone that barely carried to her ears, 'I thought I saw movement through the trees.'

He moved away, and she took a deep breath that sounded like a sob. If she'd had any remaining doubts about his motives for the farce of their engagement, his actions had destroyed them.

'What did you think it might be?' she asked steadily.

He shrugged. 'I thought it was probably a bird,' he said,

'but I wasn't sure.' He glanced around and took her hand. 'Come on. Stay close to me.'

The eerie stillness of the clearing seemed alive, as though eyes watched them all the way back to the horses. Once they were there he said, 'It was almost certainly a bird, but promise me you won't go outside the castle by yourself.'

'I won't.' She shivered. 'It's so quiet.'

He gave her a keen glance, and unexpectedly slipped his arm around her shoulders to hug her close. 'It's an uncanny place, but we Considines believe that we're safe here.'

Like that, his strength at her command, she felt safe too. And then desolate when he let her go to throw her up into the saddle. Jacoba watched him mount, eyes following the flexing, powerful muscles in his shoulders. The chill beneath her ribs dissolved into a pool of heat.

The following week she was presented to the people of the valley as Prince Marco's chosen bride, and, although she understood the motives for the very public display of possessiveness on his part, playing the part of an adoring lover hurt her deeply.

To Jacoba's astonishment, Hawke arrived at the castle on the second day, bringing Princess Melissa, so happy that she radiated it.

'So it worked out for you,' Jacoba said to him after dinner. 'I'm glad.'

He glanced at the princess, and smiled. 'It worked out,' he said. 'And for you?'

She returned his smile with a glowing one of her own. 'As you see,' she said brightly, acting for all she was worth. 'When do you announce your engagement?'

'In about a month's time. We decided yours was more important.'

She glanced at him, saw his understanding and gave him

a bleak smile. As if she'd signalled to him, Marco crossed the gracious wood-panelled room and looped an arm around her shoulder.

He was an excellent actor, she thought, heart splintering as she wished that things were different...

The family were gathering—the next arrival being Gabe's fiancée, Sara Milton, a serene woman with an innate sense of style that made her an excellent decorator. On the following day they all flew to the capital for a royal reception in the castle there. Judging by the waves from the locals and the cheering and the smiles, the occasion was a huge success.

Jacoba liked the royal couple, Prince Alex and his charming wife, Ianthe, a New Zealander who'd made a name for herself studying the dolphins in the huge lake a few miles away. She enjoyed the three small children in the nursery, two chatty little princesses and a tearaway of a crown prince.

In fact, she liked everything about Illyria, she thought, and once again found herself futilely wishing that things had happened differently. On the surface Marco was the perfect lover, but she sensed a difference in him, a distancing that hurt her beyond bearing.

They stayed in the capital city until she and Marco drove to the airport to fly to London and the launch of the perfume. Jacoba gazed at the early-morning city, red-roofed and bright in the sun, and asked, 'How do you think things went?'

'Very well. You're a hit with the family.'

His tone was so noncommittal she looked across at him, her eyes anxiously searching his face. 'You're sure Lexie will be safe when she comes?'

Her sister was finishing her tour of the Outback; after the ball in London Marco would escort Jacoba back to the Wolf's Lair and then go on to collect Lexie.

'Nothing is certain,' he said, 'but now that the news of her paternity is out, she'll be safer with us than anywhere else.'

'So it—the plan—everything—seems to be working.'

He nodded, scanning her face. 'I think our engagement is doing something that the rule of law can't do—it's making the cessation of feudal revenge emotionally satisfying.'

A note in his voice warned her that she wasn't going to like where this was leading. 'But?' she prompted.

Coolly, unemotionally, he said, 'But I suspect that an engagement won't suffice.'

An icy dread licked down her spine. 'I don't think I understand.'

'We're going to have to marry.'

The more Jacoba saw of the poverty and the tough courage of the people, their good humour and gritty determination to overcome the dictator's dark legacy, the more she admired them. She understood why Marco and his family were so uncompromisingly dedicated to helping them.

But being with him, enduring his falsely tender concern for her, his smiles and touches and his presence, had been hell. The love she'd discovered seven days previously seemed weak and childish now she'd had time to learn something of the real man, to discover the pragmatic compassion beneath the autocratic veneer.

Marriage to him would be an anguish of frustrated love, of forlorn hope that would never be assuaged. She couldn't bear it, she thought, staring out at the country that held all his loyalty.

Thinly she said, 'Is this also a decision of Prince Alex's and the council?'

She kept her face turned away from him, so he was able to study her profile. She always looked perfect in the classical clothes she favoured, sleekly expensive and elegant, and this morning she'd pulled her hair back from her face to reveal her exquisite features.

His gut contracted as though at a blow, closely followed by a surge of reckless sexual drive.

How the hell had she managed to strip him of his normal male interest in other women? Before he'd found out who she was he'd tried to push her from his mind, even instigating an intimate dinner in London with a woman he both liked and admired. They'd had a very pleasant evening with good conversation and laughter; he'd been able to fool himself that he wanted her.

Only to leave her surprised and disappointed on her doorstep.

Now all he wanted was to take Jacoba to bed and spend hours—no, damn it, *days* with her there. He despised himself for being in thrall to a primitive hunger as uncivilised as it was powerful.

She wanted him too, but she wasn't any happier than he was at the thought of marriage. Her soft, full lips were compressed, and a tiny frown had appeared between her brows.

Marco hardened his heart. He said, 'No. My own reading of the situation. I was too sanguine about an engagement doing the trick; as we've travelled around, I've felt that the only way to convince people that we're serious about this is to marry.'

White-faced, she said, 'And stay married?'

'Yes.' He took her hand, feeling the sudden leap of her pulse beneath his thumb. 'Would it be so difficult?'

The car slowed to avoid an old man, stooped and slow, driving a donkey. He looked up, and recognised the car. A smile split his face and he waved. Jacoba could have screamed. He had no right to be there, undermining her conviction that she should refuse to even entertain the idea.

'You're bound by duty, aren't you?' she said bitterly as the car picked up speed again.

'Yes. And, like me, you owe these people.'

She flashed a furious glance at his hard face. 'I know,' she said, and felt hot tears well into her eyes. 'So yes, I'll marry you—for their sake, and for Lexie's.'

His hand tightened on hers, and then released it. Very formally he said, 'I'll try to be a good husband to you. I certainly won't be unfaithful.'

'Neither will I,' she said quietly, relinquishing the last of her hopes. After all, she wouldn't be the first woman who'd married a Considine for reasons of state.

Instead of the modern penthouse apartment she'd suspected the prince might live in, he'd chosen one of a set of superb Georgian townhouses.

Well, with his heritage she shouldn't have been surprised.

'Your clothes have already been transferred here,' he said, showing her to her bedroom. 'I believe it will take you most of the day to get ready for the ball. I'll be at the office.'

In a way, that was a relief. The ball would be a spectacular occasion to benefit a charity that provided a psychological boost to women suffering the ravages of illness by organising and donating demonstrations of cosmetics. Invitations had been sent to everyone who was anyone.

And everyone had accepted; already people were talking about the party of the year.

It didn't take her most of the day to get ready, and butterflies flocked around her stomach as she sat in her bedroom waiting for Marco to knock on the door. She'd reprised the crimson ballgown she'd worn for the video shoot, with her hair piled high and cosmetics applied by her favourite expert.

Now she was assailed by an uneasy foreboding, an emptiness that felt like the precursor of panic.

It would, she thought fiercely, be so much easier to break free of this degrading desperation of desire if it were one-sided.

Whenever they were together that wild heat burned her; whenever she met Marco's eyes she saw fire in ice, a hunger that restraint only served to feed.

But there was more to it than undiluted lust, reluctant though she was to admit it. She found his presence keenly stimulating, relished crossing swords with him in conversation—she even liked the way his tone gentled when he spoke of his sister...

And then she heard his voice. She took a deep breath and opened the door to him and another man—a security man who carried a locked bag.

Marco filled her gaze, and something in her snapped, shattered. He looked—different, she thought wildly, but she didn't have time to work out what the difference was.

He held her eyes for a moment's intent scrutiny, then said quietly, 'That dress and you were made for each other.'

Her heart jumping, Jacoba said, 'Thank you.'

Excitement clawed her as the guard unlocked the bag.

'Thank you,' Marco said, and opened the case that held the necklace. 'Do you need help?'

'No.' Her voice sounded thin and taut. 'It slips over my head.'

She took the exquisite chain of fire and ice and walked across to the mirror. Marco brought across the earrings, watching as she settled the necklace into place. The earrings followed.

'I'll put this on,' he said, and positioned the tiara, arrogant features absorbed. 'Does it need pinning?'

'No.' In spite of the security guard, the intimacy of the moment sent rills of intense emotion through her. She cleared her throat, and lifted her hands to settle the tiara. 'My hair keeps it in place—see?' She summoned a smile that felt as fake as she was. 'I can't do any wild dancing, but it's steady.'

Their eyes met in the mirror, his narrowed into steel-blue

slivers, hers dark and shadowed. Jacoba's breath stopped in her throat; for a long second she heard nothing but the pulse of her blood through her veins, felt nothing but bitter-sweet joy at his closeness.

It took every bit of will-power she possessed to look away, blindly reach for the gloves and try to lose herself in the task of putting them on.

Marco forced himself to breathe slowly, to tamp down the heated rush of emotion that clouded his brain with intoxicating fumes.

She was magnificent, a woman out of a fairy tale, dangerous and provocative and ethereally beautiful, the crimson silk moulding her narrow waist and hips, her bare shoulders creamy in the lights.

Desire ached like pain through him. She glanced up as though his thoughts had manifested themselves, and swift, fugitive colour tinged her skin. For another long moment their eyes locked and held in the mirror.

'Ready?' he asked, breaking the taut silence.

'Yes.' She smoothed the fingers of her gloves.

He picked up the silk cape hanging on the back of the chair, and dropped it over her shoulders. 'Then let's go.'

In the limousine, with the security guard in front, she commented in a remote voice, 'I hope you had a good day.'

He turned his head and looked at her elegant profile, the soft lips full and provocative in the lights of London.

'An excellent one, thank you. Perhaps because I'm feeling rather pleased with life at the moment,' he said casually, and reached across to take her hand, folding his fingers around hers.

Jacoba's heart jumped. She sent him a startled glance before hastily turning her face towards the road again, thoughts scrambling through her brain.

What did he mean? He looked as arrogant and uncompromising as ever, but something in his tone told her that his very suspect pleasure was related to her.

She risked another sideways glance. Perhaps it was a trick of the lights outside that tinged his smile with tenderness; a wistful hope burgeoned into life as, hand-locked and silent like lovers sealing a pact, they journeyed through the streets of London to the venue.

Where they were faced with a barrage of flashlights and more than a few intrusive questions. Jacoba forced herself into business mode, ignoring the more cheeky of the questions, answering the ones directed at her, listening with a smile to Marco's adroit handling of those aimed at him.

But the one that hurt was directed at her.

'Is it true that your engagement is a publicity stunt to rev up hype about the new perfume?' one hard-bitten journalist asked on a slight sneer.

She lifted her brows and said, 'Grow up.'

Marco said smoothly, 'If you can't tell the difference between publicity and real life, you're in the wrong job.'

'Then how about a kiss? Just to prove it.'

Marco took Jacoba's hand. 'We don't have to prove anything,' he said caustically, and escorted her into the venue.

Once inside she gazed around the huge room, each table a small golden oasis lit by candles, the ceiling studded by fairy lights to look like stars—even the same type of huge Venetian chandelier used in the shoot.

'It looks very much more the real thing,' she said as they moved towards their table.

'I was surprised at how much like the real thing the restaurant at the top of the ski lift looked,' Marco replied, his voice deep and sure and surprisingly reassuring.

'Me too,' she said ungrammatically. 'But that's modern film-making for you—the theatre of illusion.'

'Like so much in modern life.' He changed the subject. 'You're wearing the perfume, I notice.'

She'd been given a tiny phial of the precious stuff. 'Of course. I notice there's some for every woman here. When will we learn the name?'

'After the video's been shown.'

Of course, the evening went smoothly; it wouldn't dare do anything else with the prince in charge. The food was superb, the wine magnificent and Marco's witty speech short.

At the end of it he turned to her and reached out a hand. 'Ladies and gentleman, I give you the face of *Princessa*— Jacoba Sinclair.'

The Illyrian word for princess! As applause swelled in the ballroom, she rose to stand beside him and swept a full court curtsey, a smile pinned to her face while he briefly praised her part in the video with humour and style.

A representative of the charity spoke with heartfelt passion, and then the lights were dimmed and on the huge screen the video was presented.

It was the first time she'd seen it in its entirety; she watched keenly, relaxing only when it became obvious that the scenes in the ski restaurant had been replaced entirely with the later shots from the warehouse in Auckland. She was relieved; she didn't want the world to see her face when she'd danced with Marco for the first time.

After the applause died down, the band struck up a waltz.

'Our dance,' Marco said, getting to his feet.

Ignoring the flash of cameras, Jacoba went into his arms, every cell in her body tense and expectant, keeping her gaze fixed on the dancers behind.

She surprised herself by asking suddenly, 'Do you ever think that the money that's paying for this could be better spent?'

'Naturally,' Marco said evenly. 'All of this is for one thing only—to earn enough money to give the people of Illyria their chance to enter the modern world. There are spin-offs, of course—not least the pleasure the perfume will give to millions of women—' he paused before finishing on a note that made her catch her breath '—and their men.'

'Is that why you're pulling out all the stops for this promotion?'

He was silent a moment before saying, 'Yes. But also because when I do something I like to do it well. Like you.'

From beneath long lashes she sent him a startled glance. 'How do you know that?'

His shoulder moved beneath her hand. 'I watched you while you were shooting. You had your own suggestions, even though the director resented them, and you gave it everything you had. Have you thought of being an actress?'

Trying to hide the cynical note in her voice, she said, 'No. I get bored too easily. And filming is long periods of boredom.'

'So what were you planning to do with your life once you gave up modelling?'

A slow, subtle tension was building inside her, sweet and fierce and dangerous. She said quietly, 'I was going back to New Zealand to write books.'

'Books?'

'Children's books. And adult books, if I can.' She kept her gaze fixed on the whirl of colour as the dancers swayed and dipped, the women's exquisite dresses and jewels emphasised by the black and white of their partners' evening clothes. 'I've already had two young-adult books published.'

That startled him, she was pleased to see.

'A very talented woman,' he said evenly. 'Why have I not heard of them?'

'Possibly because you're not a young adult, but also because I publish under another name. And no,' she added before he could ask, 'it's not that I'm ashamed of them. I didn't want notoriety value; I wanted them to be accepted on their own merits.'

'Very worthy. Are they?'

'They're selling well,' she said calmly. 'And got mostly excellent reviews.'

Whenever she was with Marco she had to resist the urge to confide in him, even though she knew he had little interest in the real person behind the glamorous body. Oh, he wanted her; he enjoyed her company. But in Illyria she'd realised that his first loyalty would always be to his country.

Whereas she was fascinated and intrigued by him. The goad of sexuality was always there—forbidden, heated and reckless—but each day she was with him she felt her love deepen—a love that would never be reciprocated. And she had no way of protecting herself.

Marriage would mean surrendering everything that was hers.

It was an oddly moving moment; she was torn by conflicting emotions—glory in the knowledge of love, and pain because there could be no happy ending, not even in the physical surcease of passion.

Another couple veered too close to them, their loud laughter indicating an over-indulgence in champagne. Without missing a step, Marco gathered her against his strong body, shielding her from any chance contact with the out-of-control pair.

Her breath stopped in her lungs. Locked in his arms, their steps matching perfectly, she felt that bone-deep security again.

'All right?' he said, somehow managing to imbue the ordinary words with a profoundly sexy intonation.

'Fine, thank you.' Her voice sounded distant, almost impersonal, but nobody and nothing, she thought dreamily, would ever be able to take these precious moments from her.

He didn't relax his hold, and they stayed silent until the music drew to a close and he took her back to their table, stopping on the way to receive congratulations.

An enormous tiredness drained her; she straightened her shoulders and forced herself to concentrate, to smile and smile and smile, to dance with every male at the VIP table, to look as though she was enjoying herself.

Eventually the evening wound down. Once they reached his townhouse her forbidden eagerness kicked into feverish anticipation, licking through her like honeyed fire while the jewellery was packed away and the guard took his leave.

She said formally, 'It's been a wonderful evening, and I'm sure the perfume will sell hugely. The name is inspired.'

'Thank you,' Marco said, but absently, his face hard and almost drawn, as though the late night had dimmed his splendid vitality.

No, she thought dazedly, looking up at him, he wasn't tired; he was concentrating fully on her, and his intention was suddenly plain.

Excitement beat high through her, bringing swift heat to her skin. Her mouth felt tender and full, as though he'd already kissed her, and her body—oh, her body *hungered*, with such force that she found herself swaying towards him in surrender.

CHAPTER ELEVEN

'MARCO, this is not a good idea,' Jacoba heard herself say in a thin, stark voice.

'I know, but right now it seems to be the only idea my brain can come up with.' His voice was harsh and raw, each word a statement of need so intense that it shivered through her.

When she made the mistake of looking at him, she almost cried aloud at the hunger that hardened his features into an antique mask of passion. Something broke inside her, splintering every good resolution, every wary foreboding.

Yet he didn't touch her. Eyes burnished and intent, he said softly, 'You drive me crazy! I watched you dancing, and every time any man looked at you I wanted to hit him!'

Starkly honest, she admitted, 'It works both ways, that craziness.'

And then, when the tension was spiralling out of control, he reached for her, holding her against him as though for those long moments just the feel of her was enough. His arms loosened a little, but as the first pang of frustrated disappointment struck, he bent his head and kissed the sensitive spot where her neck joined her shoulder, and then bit it gently, his strong teeth sending erotic chills shuddering through her.

Instantly he froze. 'Did I hurt you?' he demanded.

'No.'

But he kissed her skin again, his mouth tender. Jacoba had to stop herself from tearing his tie free and wrenching his shirt open. This, she realized, was what she'd been waiting for all evening—ever since they'd first made love.

Her silent sigh converted to a gasp when he slid the fastener down the back of her ballgown, loosening the boned, strapless bodice so that it fell to her waist in a swathe of silk.

Jacoba watched his gaze darken when he took in her high, proud breasts, their rosy centres already peaking.

He closed his eyes, only opening them once he'd won a brutal internal battle against his instincts. 'Come with me,' he said in a voice she didn't recognise.

'Yes.' Anywhere, she thought.

He didn't touch her as they went into her bedroom. Once there, he stood a moment, looking down at her with eyes that glittered like crystals heated by a blue flame. 'A very fragrant, silken armful,' he said, the words flowing over her skin like a caress.

Then he kissed her, pushing the ball-dress down so that it collapsed around her feet in a crimson rustle, leaving her exposed in her satin briefs and whisper-sheer stockings.

Colour washed through her skin; he reached out a hand and helped her step out over the dress. 'I wonder what is so erotic about suspender belts?' he said, his voice rasping as he took in her sleek, elegant body, fixing finally on her high-heeled gold sandals.

'You tell me.' Her voice was slow and languid.

He smiled, heavy black lashes hiding his eyes. 'God knows,' he said. 'Perhaps the same thing that is so erotic about hair as red as a tropical sunset, and creamy skin, and eyes like a drift of smoke against a blue sky…'

As he spoke he pulled her towards him, but when she resisted he stopped, eyes hardening. 'What is it?'

She gestured at him. 'You're still dressed.'

Laughing deep in his throat, he let her go and whipped off the superbly tailored jacket and shirt, letting his tie drop to the ground, muscles rippling like oiled silk as he stooped to remove his shoes and socks. Then he pushed down his trousers, taking his briefs with them, and stood like some magnificent bronze statue from ancient times, tall and powerful and extremely aroused.

Almost, Jacoba thought, her throat tightening with ardent appreciation, as aroused as she was.

Marco thought he had never seen anything more breathtaking as she stalked towards him in her high heels. She stopped half a pace away and looked up from beneath her dark lashes, her sultry gaze clouded by reckless, open hunger.

His hands clenched involuntarily into fists at his sides when she leaned forward and placed her palm over his heart, her expression absorbed and intent. 'When you touch me I lose my mind,' she whispered, looking at her long, elegant fingers on his skin, feeling his heartbeat drive with staccato emphasis into her palm.

He said quietly, 'You do it to me too. Look.' He held out a hand. It trembled with the force of his self-control. 'I want to snatch you up and take you without finesse, lose myself in you and make you mine. I've always considered myself to be civilised. I know passion means nothing when it's not ceded freely and with an open heart, but all my body knows is that it needs you, wants something that only you can give me.'

Although the words sounded trite to him, colour danced across her cheekbones. She smiled, and in that slow, enchanting smile he saw the eager, intoxicating knowledge of power shared by all the goddesses who'd once lived around the ancient Mediterranean, women who'd spun spells and given delight and caused wars—Helen of Troy, Calypso, Venus…

Then she took his hand and guided it to rest above her heart. 'Yes,' she said simply, and went into his arms as though she belonged there.

She kicked off her shoes when he lifted her again, but she didn't get a chance to shed the last scrap of satin. Once on her bed, Marco bent his black head to her breasts, his mouth closing warmly around one urgent peak, and sucked until the nipple was tight and red.

Sensation as pure and as keen as pain transfixed Jacoba; she arched against him, one huge ache of desperate longing when he transferred his attention to the other pleading breast.

It was heaven—and she shouldn't be allowing any of it to happen, but she couldn't stop. Pleasure flooded through her, robbing her of the energy to do anything more than cling to him.

She banished thought, letting herself float in the powerful surge of mutual passion. But that iron-bound discipline of his hadn't been breached. An ember of rebellion flamed into life; this time he'd learn what it was like to lose control as completely as she did.

Jacoba let her instincts take over, running her hands across his skin, fingertips lingering on each smooth, bulge and curve, each clean, taut line of his powerful body, until she heard his breathing alter, become as harsh and erratic as hers.

He said something under his breath. Even as she looked up into his face, drawn and savage with restraint, she saw him leash his passion, use the considerable force of his will to restrain the untamed beast that looked out for a moment from his eyes.

'Wolf,' she said aloud, her voice dreamy. 'Now I see why it's the animal of your house.'

'Gabe is the wolf.' His voice was thick and a muscle beat rapidly against his arrogant jaw-line.

'You can't escape destiny…' Smiling, she cupped him with her hands, stroking so lightly that he could barely feel it. His skin was hot and smooth, the strong shaft strange to her and yet utterly familiar.

He froze, dragging in a jagged breath before saying between clenched teeth, 'Jacoba, no…'

'Lie there,' she said in a sultry little whisper. 'Let me take you this time.'

His eyes narrowed into slits, then opened, glittering and frustrated. 'If you're prepared to take the consequences as well,' he said harshly.

'I'll enjoy them.'

She bent and began to kiss him again, listening to the primal instincts that told her when he was aroused, when he relaxed, when something she did drove him almost to the edge—and while she stoked his fires, she was doing the same to her own.

In the end he lay rigid on the bed, his hands knotted in the sheets with the effort it took him not to respond to her, his teeth so tight she thought his arrogant jaw might snap. Only then did she shimmy out of her briefs and lower herself over him. With a strange little sound of yearning, she stretched out along his length and surrendered the power he'd given her.

The guttural sound at the back of his throat and the quick, explosive thrust of his body into hers whetted her pent-up hunger and sent her sky-rocketing into ecstasy.

Marco followed, his arms clamping around her, big body shuddering. Locked together, they rode the storm into a blazing release,

Long minutes later she said in a drained voice, 'I didn't believe humans could fly.'

His chest lifted, and she realised he was smiling. 'Neither did I,' he said. 'Sleep now, my heart.'

It claimed her like a black void, devouring her, but some time towards morning she woke. Marco was still beside her, his breathing slow and regular, the heat from his body reaching across the few inches that separated them.

Jacoba longed to touch him, but she didn't dare; she had no right. Although they were engaged—and she'd agreed to marry him—he had given her nothing beyond the powerful pleasure of his body; they had made no emotional commitment.

Of all the men in all the world, she thought sombrely, she had to fall in love with Prince Marco Considine. How was she going to keep her spirit intact when she longed so ardently for his love in return?

She lay for long minutes listening to the night noises of the city, a low hum that never stopped. Here, in one of the biggest cities in the world, beside the man she loved, her career at its peak and her financial future assured, she had never felt so lonely, so lost and afraid.

In the end, staring into the darkness with dry, aching eyes, she realised that she simply had to endure. Her mouth contracted into a painful grimace. After all, she wasn't the first woman to have to face this. There would be plenty in Marco's illustrious bloodline who'd married for convenient reasons.

And he too had reason to wish things were different. He was sacrificing himself for his people, hoping that it would change their attitude. For her it was more personal; she wanted Lexie safe.

And they had this—this overwhelming sexual joy. Some day there would be children. She respected him. She thought he was learning to respect her. In time they'd build a solid foundation, and she'd stop longing for the sun and the moon and the stars…

Tears clogged her throat.

'What's the matter?' he said, startling her with his raspy, early-morning voice.

'Nothing.' Desperate for him not to see her wet eyes, she turned towards him and buried her face in his throat. 'Nothing,' she repeated, because nothing could ever hurt her when she was in his arms.

They closed around her and he began to kiss her—slowly, tenderly, with a passionate craving that matched her own.

This time it was slow and piercingly sweet, and when at last it was over and they were lying in rapturous fulfilment, she thought fiercely that this had to be enough.

They slept some more, waking as the autumn sun poked weak, unenthusiastic rays through her window.

Jacoba sat up, every muscle deliciously aching. Heat colouring her skin, she hauled the sheet up with her. 'I need a shower.'

He was clearly far more accustomed to waking in a strange bed than she was to having a strange man in hers. Totally relaxed, he examined her through lowered lashes, through which she was certain she could see amusement.

'It's through the door,' he said, nodding to one on the other side of the room. 'Your wrap is in the wardrobe. I'll shower in my bathroom and collect you for breakfast. We're due to pick up the plane at ten.'

Back in his own room Marco found himself smiling at her endearing shyness. Had she been a virgin when they first made love? It didn't seem likely, and it wasn't important anyway, but he resented the ferocious stab of jealousy the thought produced. He had never been jealous before; it was another indication of the contrast between his feelings for the other women who'd shared his bed and his life for a while, and Jacoba.

She was simply—different. If they'd met with none of this baggage from the past... Ruthlessly, he cleared the thought from his brain. Fate had dealt them their hands and they had to play them out.

Showered and dressed, he decided he needed a few days away from her to clear his head. Something had shifted in their relationship, and he couldn't work out what.

Love? His mouth twisted. He'd always been determined to love sensibly; his parents' marriage had been unhappy, so he'd been cautious, looking for more than a beautiful face and seductive body in any prospective bride.

But hell, nothing about his relationship with Jacoba was *sensible*. She'd collided with his life like a kind of divine madness, astonishing and unnerving him with his total loss of control whenever he looked at her or touched her.

Leaving his room, he thought grimly that he didn't have to touch or see her—even thinking about her wrecked the logic and intelligence he'd lived his life by, and therefore his perception of himself. She'd turned his world upside down—and, although he wanted her beyond bearing, he still understood little of the real Jacoba Sinclair beyond the fact that she was gracious and generous both in bed and in her life, and had lied by implication, if not in actual fact, about her true identity.

Because she'd been acutely fearful for her sister.

She had every reason to be, he thought grimly. Lexie—real name Alexia Considine—was in real danger, yet another complication in the huge task of helping to reshape the land of his forefathers into a twenty-first century democracy.

Frowning, Jacoba said, 'I think I should go with you. She's my sister.'

'That's why you can't come,' Marco returned impatiently. 'You're a celebrity, and the less fuss the better.' His expression relaxed and he viewed her mutinous face with an indulgent smile. 'Besides, I want you safely tucked up here in the Wolf's Lair while I collect Lexie.'

Forced to agree, she bit her lip. Pushing his advantage, he

went on, 'Don't worry. We'll travel by private jet, and with any luck we'll be back before anyone realises I've gone. I've appointed a bodyguard to go with you whenever you leave the castle, but I'd be grateful if you stayed inside.'

She sent him a glinting, angry glance, but nodded. 'I hope we aren't going to spend the rest of our lives shut up here.'

'You know you won't,' he said, smiling now that he'd got his way. He held out his hand, and reluctantly she took it and let herself be pulled into his arms. He didn't try to kiss her; instead he rested his cheek on her head.

'Miss me,' he said in a deep voice that sent little shivers down her spine.

'You know I will.'

But would he miss her? She had no idea what he felt for her—whether this was his technique with his mistresses, or whether he felt something different for her. Loving him as she did, she couldn't suppress her hope that it might be the latter.

He'd promised that Lexie would be safer if the Considines accepted her, and she believed him, but an inchoate foreboding made her shiver.

She hugged him fiercely. 'Take care,' she said quietly, and at last he kissed her, tearing himself away with reluctance so obvious that it kept her sane during the following days in the Wolf's Lair. With everyone away, she wondered if this was to be her fate—alone and lonely in a strange place.

'Self-pitying wrench!' she scolded. Disgusted with herself, she decided to learn as much as she could about the country and the family that had ruled it for so long.

The housekeeper, Marya, understood and eagerly seconded her decision. She took Jacoba under her wing, showing her the apartments in the castle, most still appallingly decorated by the dictator.

'They'll soon be redecorated. The lady Sara has great plans

for them,' the elderly woman said with satisfaction on the day Marco and Lexie were due. She smiled when she saw Jacoba frown at a repulsive clock set in the stomach of a naked woman. 'It will be another two hours before Prince Marco and your sister arrive, so why don't you have a swim? It will help pass the time.'

It would. 'Good idea,' Jacoba said.

The swimming pool took up what had once been the castle jousting ground. A lonely little tower that used to be the dovecote looked down on the area. 'Prince Gabriele intends to convert it into a summer house one day,' Marya had told her, 'but it's empty now. We store the deckchairs and the loungers there in winter.'

Jacoba swam until she was exhausted, then towelled herself dry and looked up at the castle. Marco had told her it had never been taken, and she could see why; its high stone walls towered above the valley. Lexie would be safe here—but she couldn't stay here the rest of her life!

God, she hoped Marco and his brothers and their cousin the prince who ruled this lovely place were all correct when they assumed that recognising Lexie as a Considine would make her safe!

She shivered, skin prickling. It was stupid to feel that someone was watching her. Possibly someone was; a maid from one of the narrow windows, or even Marya. But eventually the eerie feeling drove her to her feet. Picking up her towels, she walked towards the little tower that had once held doves. She'd been charmed by the idea of Marco's warlike ancestors enjoying such symbols of peace, until Marya had explained that the doves were used as meat during the winters.

Of course their lives, and the lives of those who followed them, depended on such blunt pragmatism. She wandered around to a small enclave of lawn and flowerbeds, overlooked only by the windows from the little tower. Its grass and flowers were a soothing contrast to the overt might of stone walls and crenellations.

She bent to smell a rose, and someone poked something into the small of her back and a male voice said in guttural Illyrian, 'If you cry out I will kill you. Walk towards the door of the tower.'

Sheer shock froze her until a sudden shove hurtled her towards the door.

It took a moment or two for the panic to die enough for her to be able to say, 'Who are you? What do you want with me?'

Her voice shook, but the words were clear enough.

'Get inside,' he muttered, the barrel of the pistol digging into her spine.

Gathering her courage, she stopped. 'I'm not going in there,' she croaked. 'It's dark.'

'And are you afraid of the dark, you redheaded witch?' he sneered, pushing her on without compunction. 'Good.'

Mind racing, she knew that once inside she had little chance. If she screamed—but no, even the most piercing scream would be muffled by the solid stone between her and the castle. Moving as slowly as she dared, she said, 'I want to know where you're taking me.'

'To hell,' he said after a second. 'To join your traitor of a mother and the man who killed your father and mine.'

'Well, you can shoot me out here in the sunlight,' she said. Too late to wish she'd learned some sort of self-defence, but she wasn't going to walk meekly to her own death.

Adrenalin pounding through her veins, she whirled around with flailing arms and clenched fists. The pistol went flying— she grabbed for it, but he punched her just below the heart. Gasping, she sagged to her knees, barely conscious of him snatching up the gun. Her chest heaved as she fought for breath and her brain went numb.

'Walk, whore,' he commanded, his voice rising. 'Walk!'

It was impossible to obey. Bent double, she could barely hear him through the roaring in her ears and the sound of her wheezing. Dimly, she was aware of him tying her hands behind her back, and her ankles together with brutal, painful efficiency, and then he picked her up and threw her over his shoulder. She tried to knee him in the testicles, but her body was still struggling with the effects of the blow; she couldn't summon any strength to her legs.

He was immensely strong, because almost immediately they began to descend dimly lit steps that wound their way down into the darkness.

Jacoba forced herself to lie still, to recover her breath and her wits. In the second before he'd hit her, she'd seen his face. He didn't look like a murderer, she thought dazedly. But then, if murderers looked like their sins, people would know not to trust them. Hysteria gripped her; she clenched her teeth and fought it back.

He was a little taller than her, dark and good-looking in a haggard way, his face brown and weather-beaten with a scar that went from his left temple to his chin, but she suspected he was no more than ten years older than she was. But that single glance had told her that he was determined to kill her. Once he'd done that, he'd lie in wait for Lexie.

She choked back a terrified sob. No, Marco would make sure Lexie was kept safe.

Once, somewhere, she'd read that the best way to defend yourself was to make the kidnapper realise that you were a human being.

When her nausea had faded and her breath and heart had steadied, she said quietly, 'Did you hit me in the solar plexus?'

He grunted.

'It's never happened to me before,' she said. 'I thought I was going to be sick.'

Roughly her abductor said, 'It incorporates some very important nerves. There will be no lasting damage.'

Jacoba had to choke a spasm of nervous laughter. Of course there wouldn't be—in a few minutes she'd be dead. Into the silence that followed she said, 'Are you a doctor?'

He tensed, then lowered her onto a cold stone floor. The sudden movement so startled her that she cried out.

When she was silent again he snarled, 'No.' His torch swept the walls and the floor. 'It is a dungeon cell,' he explained roughly. 'Your father died here. Perhaps his ghost will come to you while you wait for death.'

'What do you mean—*wait*?' Panic thinned her voice. 'I thought you were going to shoot me.'

'I have already spent too much time here,' he said, and turned and went out, closing the door behind him to leave her in total darkness.

She cried out then but, although she heard his footsteps falter on the stone steps, he didn't come back.

At first she thought she'd go mad, but she fought panic with every weapon at her command. 'First,' she said, voice quavering into the thick darkness, 'I have to get my arms to the front. He didn't lock the door, so if I do that I might be able to untie my ankles, and then get out.'

Thanking the determination that had kept her going to the gym—and that she was naturally supple—she managed to work her legs through her arms, even though the cords cut into the skin. Eventually, after tears and grim persistence, she succeeded. Flexing her fingers, she began picking at the knots around her ankles. If only she had a light...

'You don't, so keep going,' she said firmly.

But although he'd tied them swiftly, those knots held.

Eventually, after what seemed hours, she bent her head onto her knees and wept in sheer frustration until she could cry no more.

A soft sound brought her head up. Rats, she thought on a chill of horror. Or bats? Opening her eyes to their widest, she scanned the darkness and bit her lips to stop herself from screaming. Her flesh crawled; she held her breath and strained to hear.

Eventually, when no further sound came, she relaxed and began again, working at the knots. She had to get out of here.

Had her father really died here, or had that just been a vicious twist to make her even more afraid? Her mother had told her he'd died in an ambush.

Had Paulo Considine lied to the woman he'd married?

Probably, she thought wearily, tugging hopelessly at the first knot. Incredulously she realised that it seemed a little looser, and instant hope revived her. Holding her breath, she slowed down her movements, terrified that if she pulled too hard she'd tighten the knot again. Slowly, delicately, she coaxed the loose end of cord free.

'Thank you, Papa,' she said in soft Illyrian.

The next knot was more difficult. Her fingers were tired and she was getting cold, but she forced herself to continue working until eventually it too eased free, and she could move her feet.

It took her a long time to stand; her muscles were stiff with cold and reaction, and she spent some time on her knees before she dared push upright. The blood rushed painfully through her; she gave a sharp, quick sob, and realised that she was both hungry and thirsty, and desperate to relieve herself.

She ignored everything and stumbled forward, her hands held out in front of her. The wall was cold and rough, and she whimpered when she came too abruptly to a corner and hit her head, but she had to find the door.

But when her questing hand found the heavy wood, although she groped urgently as far as she could reach, she couldn't find a handle. Desperate, she pushed with all her might, but it failed to yield.

Eventually she had to accept that there was no way out.

She collapsed into a crouch, hot tears dripping down her cheeks, utterly spent. And somehow, in spite of everything, she slept, waking to—what?

A voice—one she'd been so sure she'd never hear again.

Marco was calling, 'Jacoba. Jacoba, can you hear me?'

She had to swallow before she could answer. 'Here,' she croaked. 'Here.'

The next few minutes were a whirl of emotion; she was sobbing when he lifted her into his arms and held her clamped against his heart. 'Beloved,' he said fiercely. 'My dearest heart, are you all right?'

And then he froze. In a voice she could hardly hear, he whispered against her ear, 'Quiet. And whatever happens, don't move.'

CHAPTER TWELVE

STARK, UNBEARABLE TERROR kicked Jacoba in the stomach. She couldn't bear it if he died here with her…

Silently, he lowered her to her feet and stood between her and the dim light that bobbed towards them.

The newcomer stopped at the door of the cell.

'I do not want you, Your Highness.' It was a voice she recognised only too well. 'My business is with the redheaded witch who has caught you in her claws.'

Marco said calmly, 'You will have to kill me to get to her.'

His composure astonished and frightened Jacoba. She couldn't stop shivering and her brain was sluggish and thick, struggling to make sense of what was happening.

The man said harshly, 'I do not want to harm you, but if I have to do so, I will do it. I must kill the woman. Her mother betrayed my father's brother, and sent him to his death so that she could marry Paulo Considine.'

Still in that same calm tone Marco enquired, 'So you plan to kill your cousin?'

'She owes me the blood debt. Her father died in this cell. Her mother married the monster who killed your grandparents, may his soul rot in hell for all eternity. They are probably looking down from heaven, cursing you for making her your whore.'

'Even if that is so, what has *she* done to harm you?'

Silence. Jacoba held her breath until the man—her cousin, she realised, astonished—said fiercely, 'You should know how it is with us. Blood pays for blood. I swore to my father on his deathbed that I would collect the debt from her if she was alive.'

'So why didn't you kill her instead of bringing her here?' Marco sounded interested, not condemnatory.

The man hesitated before admitting sullenly, 'I went to shoot her, but I—could not. I am unworthy of my father's trust. But I had promised him, so I left her in the cell in which my uncle died.'

'And why did you come back?'

The man waited longer this time before speaking. Angrily he said, 'To kill her. I could not—could not let her die in the dark and alone. I would not do that to a dog, to a rat, shut up without food or water or light.' He paused. 'So I decided on a quick, clean death.'

'I suggest that you were not planning to kill her,' Marco said, his tone reflective and cool. 'I know who you are, and I have heard that you are a healer. Healers do not murder. You were going to let her go.'

Clearly agitated, the man shouted, 'I promised my father—on my knees, I promised him! He had lost everyone but me, and it was all due to that woman—her mother.'

Jacoba tensed and gripped Marco's shirt. Marco was reputed to be a born negotiator, but how could he keep his voice so steady, so level, when it was obvious the kidnapper was getting anxious? Anxious people made mistakes—like shooting the wrong person.

The thought of him dying—of all that proud male vitality brought low by a man's attempt to right an old tragedy—filled Jacoba with horror.

She'd rather die herself.

No sooner had the thought come into her head than she acted on it, hurling herself out from behind Marco with all her strength. He roared at her, a great shout of despair and rage, and grabbed her, thrusting her back so that she was protected by his body.

Into the sudden silence, another voice intervened. Marya, the housekeeper, said, 'He is right, Piero, and you know it. You came back to let her go.'

'It was well done,' Marco said. 'Because your father was wrong when he thought her mother betrayed the partisans.'

'I do not believe you,' Piero shouted furiously. 'Very well, I was going to let her go, and then I was going to kill myself, for I could not do it.'

He made a grab for his pocket, but Marco reached him before he was able to drag out the pistol, and they fought, struggling in the near-darkness. Jacoba looked around for something to clobber Piero with, but there was nothing.

And it wasn't necessary. Piero was strong, but Marco was taller and stronger; after a short, no-holds-barred struggle, he wrested the weapon from his antagonist.

'What good will killing yourself do?' he asked, breathing heavily. 'You are needed here. Marya tells me you are famous for your healing skills with animals. What will the farmers do if you die? Killing yourself is selfish.'

The beaten man said nothing. In a voice that reminded Jacoba oddly of Marco at his most high-handed, Marya said, 'Listen to me, Piero! You know me well. I do not lie, and I say to you that this woman's mother did not betray her husband or mine, or the prince's grandparents. I know this, because I killed the person who did it.'

'Who was it?' he asked hoarsely.

She made a swift, decisive gesture with her hand. 'It does not matter now. It is finished.'

Stunned, Jacoba straightened up, but the narrow cell spun about her, and she gave a low groan and crumpled. Just before unconsciousness claimed her she felt Marco's arms around her, and knew she was safe.

She woke in her bedroom, and stared at the ceiling, blinking heavily until she realised where she was. Her wrists were hurting like hell and she tried to ease them into a more comfortable position.

'You're all right—the doctor said you're dehydrated and tired and hungry, but apart from that you're fine.'

Marco's voice—and very grim he sounded. He was standing beside the bed, looking down at her.

'What doctor?' she croaked. 'I didn't think there was one in the valley.'

'I flew one in from the main hospital in the capital.'

'Thank you,' she said weakly. 'So it wasn't a dream. I'm sorry I fainted. I suppose everything just caught up with me.'

He said in a voice she'd never heard before, 'If you ever—*ever* do anything like that again, I will see to it that you can't sit down for a week.'

'Rubbish,' she said robustly, a spark of joy warming her. 'You were doing exactly the same for me—protecting me. What else could I do? He was getting nervous, and I'd rather die than have you die…'

'Why?'

A note in his voice made her look up sharply.

Their eyes locked, and she said quietly, 'Because I love you.'

He dropped to his knees and took her face in his hands, careful not to touch her bandaged wrists. Face drawn and haggard, he said, 'When Lexie and I got back here to find out that you'd been taken, I—hell, Jacoba, I nearly went mad. I thought you were dead. I'd made you come here, and promised you'd be safe.'

'It's all right,' she soothed. 'Everything's fine. As a villain, he's no great shakes.'

'Nevertheless I'm not ever going through that again,' Marco said firmly. 'We'll get married tomorrow, and then we'll get the hell out of this place and never come back.'

She closed her eyes, because the world was dizzily spinning again. 'That's taking remorse a little too far,' she croaked.

'Remorse?' he said explosively, that iron-bound control shattered completely. 'I don't want to marry you because of remorse. I've been trying not to fall in love with you, but while I was picking up Lexie I realised it was hopeless. I missed you so much. It was like leaving half of me behind. Coming back and finding you'd been taken—might even be dead—made me understand how deeply, irrevocably, painfully I love you—too late, I was sure.'

'But it wasn't,' she said wonderingly, a wild mixture of delight and relief and sheer, blatant happiness blazing so brightly within her that she couldn't stop smiling.

He laughed and kissed her mouth, gently, and then not quite so gently. Against her lips he said, 'You hold my heart and my future in your hands, my darling. If I don't have you, I have nothing.'

Tears filled her eyes. He kissed them away and said, 'But next time I tell you not to move, stay still.'

She laughed, and gulped back another sob. 'I love you desperately, and when you pushed me behind you I was frantic. He could have killed you, and you had nothing to do with the whole sordid, appalling past,' she said, remembering how useless she'd felt. 'I want to share your life, not be protected like some fragile flower that will die in a shower of rain.'

'I have to protect my heart.' But he smiled and kissed her smart retort from her lips. 'I'll try,' he whispered.

She winced as she lifted her hands to him. He took them and

kissed each palm, then got up and said with considerable irony, 'No doubt it serves me right that when I want to take you to bed so much that I might well die from wanting, I cannot.'

'You could have before,' she said tartly. 'Ever since we've got here, I've lain awake night after night, hoping that you'd come.'

'I didn't feel I had the right. I had forced you into an engagement, and then manoeuvred you into a marriage I knew you didn't want. I suppose I wanted you to have some independence.' His eyes kindled and he finished on a note that set her pulse slamming through her body, 'I was a fool.'

Drawing him down to sit on the edge of the bed, she said, 'Can we let it go, darling? I'm sick of the past; Lexie once said that we'd lived in the shadows all our lives, and she was right. Can't we all move out into the sunlight now?'

His fingers tightened around hers so that she flinched. He loosened his grip immediately and lifted her hand to his mouth, holding it there as he spoke so that each word sent a heated shiver of hunger through her. 'My dearest, will you be happy with me? We can live wherever you like, and I've already started to ease back on my workload.'

'I'll be happy wherever you are, whatever you do,' she told him simply, and smiled mistily up into his beloved face. 'I love you so much. I've been fighting it too, but—I didn't put up much of a struggle. I think I knew right from the start.'

He laughed at that, and kissed her wrist. 'As did I,' he said. 'We danced in a mock-ballroom, and by the time the night was over I owned a heart no longer. So, shall we marry with Melissa and Gabe and their lovers in a triple wedding ceremony?'

Suddenly realising what it would mean, she said worriedly, 'Are you sure?'

'More sure than I have ever been about anything,' he said, the words a vow never to be broken. 'Surer than I am that the sun will shine on us tomorrow. Surer than I am that the sea won't roll over the mountain top—even surer than I am that you love me.'

She kissed him and he lifted her carefully, tenderly, onto his lap. 'Ah, no—you know I do.'

He laughed, soft and deep and low, and locked his arms around her.

They were still like that when Marya came knocking at the door. 'All is well?' she asked, her tone and smile making it obvious she knew it was.

'Yes,' they said together.

She said, 'My lady's cousin wishes to see her.' She paused, saying somewhat hurriedly before either of them spoke, 'He is very distressed, and needs to know that he is forgiven—or at least that you understand why he felt he had to do what he did.'

Marco looked down at Jacoba's suddenly pale face. 'Do you want to see him?'

A sudden fear battled with the knowledge that she should build bridges with the man who'd locked her up and terrified her. 'Yes, all right.'

Marco hugged her. 'I'll be here. Before he comes in, I believe, and my head of security believes also, that he didn't want to kill you. If he had, he'd have shot you when he found you in the garden. Leaving you in the dungeon doesn't make sense. He must have known that the castle would be searched from the topmost turret to the deepest dungeon—and he'd also know that Marya knows it as well as she knows her own face. I think he probably wanted you to be found.'

Marya glanced at Jacoba, safe in her lover's arms, and nodded vigorously. 'Honour drove him to try to keep faith with his father, but he is a kind man. He would have been a doctor if he hadn't been targeted by the dictator.'

Marco frowned. 'Marya, you know what people are thinking. Is there likely to be any more talk of revenge or feuds?'

The old housekeeper's face grew solemn. 'I don't think so,' she said, but without her usual conviction. 'Now we have police and officials who are not corrupt, and rulers who care for us, people are beginning to realise that a feud is not the only way to get justice. Prince Alex has told everyone that revenge only creates the need for more revenge. I think people are beginning to believe him.'

Dismissing that with a gesture, Jacoba said, 'But what about Lexie? Plenty of people have reason to hate her. Even if only one person wants to kill her, she'll be a sitting target because she's Paulo Considine's daughter. After my father went to fight with the partisans, when Mama was alone and unprotected, Considine forced her into a relationship. Lexie was the result. Then, once my father was dead, he married her.'

Marco said forcibly, 'So many deaths, so many trage-dies, all caused by one man's sick ambition and all, in the end, for nothing. Paulo Considine is dead. I swear, your cousin's attempt will be the last time anyone attempts to live by the tenets of the blood feud. I'll find a way to stop it once and for all.'

He settled Jacoba back into bed and stood beside it, tall and dominant and formidable.

But the residue of fear vanished once she saw her cousin. His agony of mind was obvious. Gently, Jacoba said to him, 'Apart from my sister, you're my only relative.'

Blinking, he responded, 'I swear on the saints—on holy St Ivan himself—that I shall not try to kill your sister.' After a moment's hesitation, he went on, 'I could not carry out my father's wishes even when I had you at my mercy.'

'Because you knew they were wrong,' Marco said uncom-promisingly.

Jacoba interposed, 'You will have much in common with my sister, for she also is a veterinarian.'

He looked up eagerly, but his gaze fell. 'I'm glad I failed. Perhaps it was because the lady was watching over her family as she always has.' He bowed. 'Sir, if you wish to kill me—'

Jacoba's instant outcry blended with Marco's forceful reply. 'Your cousin isn't hurt, and I believe you when you say that you are sorry. Even if you'd killed her, I wouldn't do the same to you. I'd prosecute you with the utmost severity of the law, but killing plays no place in Illyria now. Do one thing for us—for Illyrians everywhere: speak out against blood feuds whenever and wherever you can.'

'I will,' he vowed, straight and oddly formal. He made another bow to Marco, and turned to leave.

Impetuously, Jacoba held out a hand to him. He blinked and stopped when he saw the bandage on her wrist, but when she beckoned he came up to the side of the bed. She lifted herself up and leaned forward to kiss his cheek. 'Thank you, cousin,' she said softly.

He froze, and then slowly, tentatively, he put his arm around her and kissed her forehead. Jacoba sensed his emotions, tangled and bewildered, and then he gave a huge sob and backed out of the room.

When Marya had escorted him away, Marco said softly, 'You've made another slave.'

'Nonsense,' she said, colouring. 'When he said the lady stopped him from hurting me, who did he mean?'

'The Queen, our very distant ancestor.' Marco shrugged. 'The people of the valley believe that she is still here, still watching over her children's children.'

'Do you believe it?' she said quietly.

His smile was lopsided. 'I'm a thoroughly modern man, and a cynic to boot, so I've been told more than once.'

'But?' she probed. Did he too think that Marya was not—quite—the peasant she seemed to be?

'But sometimes I think they might have something. Are you satisfied that Lexie will be safe?'

'Not—entirely,' she said soberly.

He walked across to the window and looked out over the valley, his face hardening. Heart beating unsteadily, Jacoba watched him.

Without turning his head he said, 'I feel that to scotch this once and for all we need some dramatic gesture of public reconciliation. The Illyrians are religious. Would you and Lexie be prepared to take part in a—say, a vigil in the cathedral where the relics of St Ivan, the patron saint, are held?'

When she hesitated he finished, 'You'd be guarded by sharpshooters, so you'd be safe.' And when she still said nothing he said with brutal, unsparing candour, 'No, I won't lie to you. You'd both be as safe as it is possible to make you.'

Jacoba had thought that if only Marco could love her, she'd be completely happy. Now she discovered that even such glorious relief and pleasure and hope wasn't unalloyed. Always, he'd put Illyria first, even if it meant exposing her and Lexie to danger.

But it no longer stung. Marco wouldn't be the man she loved if he could ignore his obligations.

Perhaps it was time for her to take up the burden of her heritage too. 'I'll do it,' she said quietly. 'But no soldiers, no guns. If it's to mean anything we need to be honourable about it, and to trust the people. After all, you Considines are asking them to trust you; it should be a two-way thing. As for Lexie— why don't you ask her?'

Lexie was silent for long moments when Marco had put his suggestion to her in Gabe's study. Prince Alex had been consulted; he'd checked with his council, who seized on the idea.

Gabe said, 'You don't need to do this, Lexie.'

'I think I do.' She squared her shoulders. 'He was my

father and if this is necessary to make things right for the country he trashed, I'll do it.' She looked at Jacoba. 'But you're not going to.'

'Don't be an idiot,' her older sister said stringently. 'You do it, I do it.'

She stood firm during the week that followed—a week when Prince Alex and his council prepared the people for the event.

In the end, Lexie accepted her sister's presence, although, as they were driven through the dark streets to the green and white striped cathedral, she said, 'I wish you weren't here.'

'Scared?' Jacoba asked. There were so few people in the streets the city seemed deserted.

'Yeah.' Lexie shrugged. 'But it's the only thing to do, I feel. I've been reading about the Considines—Marya's been putting me through a pretty strenuous education regime! They were big on duty.' She looked acutely self-conscious. 'I'm glad I'm one. I feel I owe it to the Illyrians to do what I can. I just hope it works.'

So did Jacoba. Both were silent as they were met at the cathedral door by the archbishop. The huge building was echoing and bare, with no flowers, the only lights the candles on the altar.

Silently the archbishop led them towards it. Jacoba felt an icy scud of foreboding down her spine. She couldn't help thinking that they'd be silhouetted against the light—perfect targets. And although it had taken Alex's intervention, they'd managed to prevail on Marco not to ring the cathedral with snipers, so they were on their own.

They both sank to their knees. Jacoba heard the soft swish of the cleric's robes as he left them there. She prayed for Illyria, for its people and its culture, for the children who'd grow up in freedom, for its well-being…

Almost immediately, soft sounds almost drove her to her feet. Her heart thudded, beating so heavily it almost drowned out the sounds of people coming quietly into the cathedral. The skin down her spine tightened, and she started to reach for Lexie's hand to drag her to her feet so that at least they'd die facing their murderers, when she realised that this was no small group.

The first quiet footsteps gave way to the shuffles of many; she sensed them come in, hundreds, perhaps thousands of them, their coughs and sighs and the slight rustle of clothes as they knelt filling the huge building. And above all, the soft sibilance of whispered prayers. The people of Illyria had come to join her and Lexie in their vigil.

Stunned and joyful, she knew then that everything was going to be all right.

But it wasn't until later, when they emerged from the cathedral, that she realised how many people had supported them. As Marco, his face sharply honed, half-carried her from the cathedral, she was astounded to see the square filled with silent, black-clad people, more kneeling in the side-streets, others obviously making their way home.

Gabe, an arm around Lexie, said quietly, 'It's been the same all over the country. The churches and chapels have been packed. It's been a huge vote of confidence in you two, but also in Alex's rule. I imagine it's marked the end of the blood feud.'

Marco's black head moved in a quick nod. 'Dictatorships are built on betrayal, on a million small treacheries every day. Lexie's relationship to Paulo Considine, which seemed an insurmountable problem, has turned out to be yet another element in bringing the country together.' He looked down at Jacoba's pale face, and his eyes heated, became intimate and crystalline. 'And you, my heart, are going to bed the moment we reach the castle.'

'All right,' she said with a yawn. 'Where were you?' When he was silent, she said, 'I know you were in the cathedral somewhere. You gave in too easily.'

Gabe snorted. 'He was in the gallery with his band of specially chosen sharpshooters.'

'I thought we'd agreed—' Lexie protested, only to be cut off by Marco.

'I told Jacoba that you'd be safe here,' he said coolly. 'So it was my responsibility to make sure you were.'

Lexie gave him a scathing look, but grinned as her eyes met her sister's astonished gaze. 'We should have known, I suppose,' she drawled.

In the palace overlooking the city they ate a light supper, and then went up to bed. Jacoba had just crawled into an old T-shirt when someone knocked on her door. Hauling on her robe, she went across to open it, unable to stop her sleepy smile when she saw Marco.

'How are you?' he asked, piercing eyes scanning her face.

'Tired, but relieved. It really did mean something, didn't it?'

'Yes.' His mouth compressed. 'I loved you before, but last night—I've never admired a woman so much. It took a huge amount of courage to do what you and Lexie did. And it worked. Just before I came up, Alex got word that the killer who was acquitted after the last feud handed himself in to the police this morning.'

'That's wonderful!' she said, her face lighting up.

'My beautiful heroine,' he said, and kissed her. 'My love—my dearest heart—I adore you.'

She clung, and kissed him back, relief and an indefinable lightness of spirit making her even more giddy than his kisses. When she could breathe again, she said, 'I know it's a royal tradition, but do we have to wait for a year to get married? Would it be cheating if we had a tiny wedding on the beach in New Zealand—my beach—with just Melissa and Hawke and Lexie and Gabe and Sara as witnesses? Say, in a month's time?'

His arms hardened around her. 'I can think of nothing I'd

like more, but we still need to be married here. It's part of the Illyrian constitution.'

She rested her face in the hollow of his throat, smelling the faint, sexy scent that belonged only to him. 'I'll enjoy that,' she said cheerfully. 'A woman can't have too many weddings.'

'Provided I'm the only groom in your life,' he said, his tone low and not quite threatening.

'You will be the only man in my life,' she promised quietly, her heart singing. 'Forever.'

But when he'd kissed her again, she added with a catch of infinite delight in her voice, 'Unless we have sons, of course…'

Bells rang all through the capital city, sending birds wheeling above the crowds. Beneath a brilliant sun the city buzzed as revellers enjoyed the occasion. Cafés and bars were crammed, every window and balcony was filled with onlookers trailing music and laughter.

Illyria was *en fête*, celebrating the weddings of the three Considine siblings. Those who could get to the capital lined the streets, ready to cheer until their throats were hoarse. In the countryside, people who ten years before had hardly dared to hope waited to light bonfires, prepared for a day and night of feasting and dancing while they toasted the three couples. The harvest had been excellent, and the summer had held on. People were already talking of a blessed year.

The Considines met before the ceremony, Melissa graceful in a gown cut on mediaeval lines that revealed her slender figure, the Considine tiara—resplendent in diamonds from Golconda and rubies believed by some to have been mined and polished in Atlantis—poised on her proud head.

She inspected her two brothers, tall and dark and outstandingly handsome in the full regalia of princes of Illyria. 'You look utterly gorgeous! I fully expect to see two brides swoon when they walk up the aisle in the cathedral.'

'Sara's not likely to,' Gabe said drily. 'She might look delicate, but she's made of spun steel.'

Marco grinned. 'And Jacoba's not into fainting.' Not unless she's starving and dehydrated and traumatised, he thought, his heart stopping a moment as he relived those terrifying hours when he'd thought he'd lost her forever.

Banishing the horror, he eyed his sister. Happiness had given her a radiance that still made him blink. 'I'll bet Hawke won't be able to keep that trademark cool of his when he turns to see you. Am I allowed to kiss you?'

'Of course you are!' She kissed him back. 'Are you satisfied that Jacoba and Lexie are safe?'

Marco said uncompromisingly, 'I'm satisfied, otherwise they wouldn't be riding through the streets in a carriage. The Illyrians now consider them both to be innocent victims of the past. As we all do.'

It helped, he knew, that Jacoba was beautiful and Lexie looked nothing like her father; he'd been short and stout, whereas she was tall and slender, and strikingly attractive.

Alex had made sure the whole country knew of Lexie's skill when it came to saving animals; the media had made a great fuss of her work for the peasants in the valley, and that she was learning old country remedies from Jacoba's cousin. Photographs of the various animals she'd rescued from death's door had figured largely, as had her smile, winning hearts all over the country.

Without preamble, Melissa said, 'Have you ever thought that Marya—somehow manipulates things?'

Marco looked at Gabe. She hurried on, 'I mean—common sense tells me she's simply a shrewd, heartbreakingly loyal peasant, but sometimes I've wondered if she's a witch. She has an uncanny habit of somehow being involved when things are going to happen.'

So she'd felt it too. And in spite of Gabe's poker-face, Marco had read his thoughts. You, too, he thought, still baffled by what could only be a superstitious hangover from the past.

He said, 'In the valley they believe that when Illyria needs her, the Queen who brought her treasure here and died at the standing stone is reincarnated.'

Coolly, noncommittally, Gabe spoke. 'One of those charming country legends.' He glanced at his brother.

'Who knows? I'm just glad she's on our side.'

Another peal of bells rang out from churches across the city. Melissa gave an odd, half-smothered laugh. 'So we're all desperately trying to be cool about the fact that we suspect the housekeeper at the Wolf's Lair is the reincarnation of the ancient Queen! OK, I won't say anything more about it if you don't.' Assuming an exaggerated social voice, she said, 'Don't you think it's lovely of the Illyrians to be making such a fuss when I suspect they know that this is all a farce—that we all sneaked off for secret weddings long ago?'

Both men looked indulgently at her. 'Of course they know,' Gabe said, 'but they love a party, and this is the best chance they've got until one of us produces a child. Now, shouldn't we be getting into carriages?'

The triple wedding was everything the waiting crowds longed for—a triumph. The crowds cheered Jacoba and Lexie in their white and gold carriage every bit as enthusiastically as they cheered the other two brides.

After the night in the cathedral the change in the atmosphere had been electric, so obvious that Jacoba was no longer worried. Smiling, she waved at the ecstatic crowds. Her fingers touched the earrings—part of the ancient Queen's treasure. When the two brothers had decided that each bride should wear part of the hoard, she and Melissa had decided that, as Sara was marrying the head of the family to become Grand Duchess, she should wear the Queen's Blood, the superb necklace.

'It's your family tiara,' Jacoba said to Melissa. 'So you wear it.'

'Are you sure?'

Jacoba grinned. 'I wore one for the ad campaign. They weigh a ton! I'll take the earrings, thanks very much.'

Happiness filled her; she wondered if the cheering onlookers could see it radiate from her like sunbeams. The past months had given her total confidence in Marco's love. The arrangements for the wedding had gone like a dream—the three brides had even managed to choose gowns they adored that blended together, thanks to Sara, with her designer's skill, who'd suggested a Grecian styling for them all.

Inside the cathedral the organ thundered as she walked down the aisle, her four bridesmaids—Lexie and three friends—following. Perfume from the roses that adorned the building hung heavily, blending with the *Princessa* she'd sprayed on her wrists just before she left the castle.

And that was another thing—the perfume was already being spoken of as a classic, one of the rare perfumes that lasted.

She couldn't make out the words of the hushed comments from the congregation; her attention was concentrated on Marco's tall figure, waiting for her.

Tears burned her eyes; she blinked, and the lights from the candelabra on the altar danced as more triumphant music proclaimed Melissa's arrival.

Bouquet clutched in her nervous hands, bridesmaids clustered behind her, she waited motionless as the congregation sat down and the archbishop moved regally towards Sara and Gabe.

For all the pomp and splendour, the royal guests and the power élite of the world in the congregation, the actual wedding ceremony was simple and intensely moving. Jacoba blinked back more tears as Marco's brother and his bride plighted their undying loyalty and love.

Once she caught Marco's eye and had to look away because her control over her emotions was so tenuous. She wasn't going to cry like a baby at her own wedding!

But at last their turn came. Jacoba handed over her bouquet to Lexie. Side by side, she and Marco stood together, the ancient, solemn words echoing in their ears. And Marco's hand closed around hers, warm and strong and infinitely supportive.

His voice was deep and utterly confident as he made his vows, hers soft and low but without a tremor. The rings were produced; Marco slipped the plain gold band onto her finger. Forcing herself to relax, she took his hand and did the same. Hand in hand, they listened as the archbishop pronounced them husband and wife and the music swelled and the choir's voices rose in soaring, glorious triumph.

Seated in one of the galleries, Marya smiled as Melissa and Hawke pledged their vows in turn. They were happy, her children. All she had set out to do was done. She could die tonight, knowing that the valley and Illyria were safe now, at least for another hundred years or so.

But soon there would be babies, and a new life for this place she loved almost more than she loved the family whose roots were buried deep in its soil. Her old eyes half-closed as she remembered days long ago, when she'd ridden in a litter to meet her fate.

Much later Marco ran a possessive fingertip down his wife's throat, his eyes kindling. They'd decided to honeymoon on the coast, and the old, beautiful villa was filled with the sound of the sea and the scent of flowers, and distant sounds of revelry from the village at the base of the cliffs. Sudden bursts of rockets soaring into the warm night air showed that the people were still celebrating.

He said, 'Happy?'

Wearing only her wedding ring, and still shuddering from a surfeit of pleasure, Jacoba whispered, 'I'm always happy now. You know that.'

She tightened her arms around him with the confidence born of complete security, every fear banished by his love.

'So am I,' he said quietly. 'When I wake each morning and see you beside me, sleepy and silken, that glorious hair spread out around your beloved face, your lovely smile just for me, I know that nothing in this world means as much to me as you do. Have I managed to convince you that, although I feel a huge loyalty to Illyria, I'd die for you? You will always come first in my life.'

Shaken, she kissed the spot above his heart. 'Yes. I love you so much more than I did a year ago,' she confessed. 'I didn't know that love grows and grows until it fills your life.'

A huge moon directed a flood of silver light through the unshuttered windows. Sleek and sated, Marco bent his head and made a girdle of kisses around her waist, his lips lingering against the warm satin. 'And if you're right, and that seduction scene you enacted last week means that our first child is already with us, then I'll have more than I've ever wanted.'

She smiled tremulously. 'I hope so—but there's no reason why we shouldn't make sure, is there?'

He laughed deep in his throat and reached for her. 'No reason at all,' he vowed.

Later still, when the moon had sailed westward and rockets no longer exploded like chrysanthemums in the warm night sky, she lay listening to the beating of his heart beneath her cheek.

Softly, soberly, she said, 'Lexie and I spent so much of our lives being terrified of the very word Illyria, but today in the streets the people threw flowers at us. It was like a dream.'

'A dream you and Lexie made come true with your courage,' he said uncompromisingly. 'From now on, dear heart, life will throw nothing but flowers at you.'

MILLS & BOON®

Live the emotion

JANUARY 2007 HARDBACK TITLES

ROMANCE™

Title	Author	ISBN
Royally Bedded, Regally Wedded	*Julia James*	0 263 19556 2
The Sheikh's English Bride	*Sharon Kendrick*	0 263 19557 0
Sicilian Husband, Blackmailed Bride	*Kate Walker*	0 263 19558 9
At the Greek Boss's Bidding	*Jane Porter*	0 263 19559 7
The Spaniard's Marriage Demand	*Maggie Cox*	0 263 19560 0
The Prince's Convenient Bride	*Robyn Donald*	0 263 19561 9
One-Night Baby	*Susan Stephens*	0 263 19562 7
The Rich Man's Reluctant Mistress	*Margaret Mayo*	0 263 19563 5
Cattle Rancher, Convenient Wife	*Margaret Way*	0 263 19564 3
Barefoot Bride	*Jessica Hart*	0 263 19565 1
Their Very Special Gift	*Jackie Braun*	0 263 19566 X
Her Parenthood Assignment	*Fiona Harper*	0 263 19567 8
The Maid and the Millionaire	*Myrna Mackenzie*	0 263 19568 6
The Prince and the Nanny	*Cara Colter*	0 263 19569 4
A Doctor Worth Waiting For	*Margaret McDonagh*	0 263 19570 8
Her L.A. Knight	*Lynne Marshall*	0 263 19571 6

HISTORICAL ROMANCE™

Title	Author	ISBN
Innocence and Impropriety	*Diane Gaston*	0 263 19748 4
Rogue's Widow, Gentleman's Wife	*Helen Dickson*	0 263 19749 2
High Seas to High Society	*Sophia James*	0 263 19750 6

MEDICAL ROMANCE™

Title	Author	ISBN
A Father Beyond Compare	*Alison Roberts*	0 263 19784 0
An Unexpected Proposal	*Amy Andrews*	0 263 19785 9
Sheikh Surgeon, Surprise Bride	*Josie Metcalfe*	0 263 19786 7
The Surgeon's Chosen Wife	*Fiona Lowe*	0 263 19787 5

JANUARY 2007 LARGE PRINT TITLES

ROMANCE™

Mistress Bought and Paid For *Lynne Graham*	0 263 19415 9
The Scorsolini Marriage Bargain *Lucy Monroe*	0 263 19416 7
Stay Through the Night *Anne Mather*	0 263 19417 5
Bride of Desire *Sara Craven*	0 263 19418 3
Married Under the Italian Sun *Lucy Gordon*	0 263 19419 1
The Rebel Prince *Raye Morgan*	0 263 19420 5
Accepting the Boss's Proposal *Natasha Oakley*	0 263 19421 3
The Sheikh's Guarded Heart *Liz Fielding*	0 263 19422 1

HISTORICAL ROMANCE™

The Bride's Seduction *Louise Allen*	0 263 19379 9
A Scandalous Situation *Patricia Frances Rowell*	0 263 19380 2
The Warlord's Mistress *Juliet Landon*	0 263 19381 0

MEDICAL ROMANCE™

The Midwife's Special Delivery *Carol Marinelli*	0 263 19331 4
A Baby of His Own *Jennifer Taylor*	0 263 19332 2
A Nurse Worth Waiting For *Gill Sanderson*	0 263 19333 0
The London Doctor *Joanna Neil*	0 263 19334 9
Emergency in Alaska *Dianne Drake*	0 263 19531 7
Pregnant on Arrival *Fiona Lowe*	0 263 19532 5

MILLS & BOON®

Live the emotion

FEBRUARY 2007 HARDBACK TITLES

ROMANCE™

The Marriage Possession *Helen Bianchin*	978 0 263 19572 9
The Sheikh's Unwilling Wife *Sharon Kendrick*	978 0 263 19573 6
The Italian's Inexperienced Mistress *Lynne Graham*	
	978 0 263 19574 3
The Sicilian's Virgin Bride *Sarah Morgan*	978 0 263 19575 0
The Rich Man's Bride *Catherine George*	978 0 263 19576 7
Wife by Contract, Mistress by Demand *Carole Mortimer*	
	978 0 263 19577 4
Wife by Approval *Lee Wilkinson*	978 0 263 19578 1
The Sheikh's Ransomed Bride *Annie West*	978 0 263 19579 8
Raising the Rancher's Family *Patricia Thayer*	978 0 263 19580 4
Matrimony with His Majesty *Rebecca Winters*	978 0 263 19581 1
In the Heart of the Outback... *Barbara Hannay*	978 0 263 19582 8
Rescued: Mother-To-Be *Trish Wylie*	978 0 263 19583 5
The Sheikh's Reluctant Bride *Teresa Southwick*	
	978 0 263 19584 2
Marriage for Baby *Melissa McClone*	978 0 263 19585 9
City Doctor, Country Bride *Abigail Gordon*	978 0 263 19586 6
The Emergency Doctor's Daughter *Lucy Clark*	978 0 263 19587 3

HISTORICAL ROMANCE™

A Most Unconventional Courtship *Louise Allen*	978 0 263 19751 8
A Worthy Gentleman *Anne Herries*	978 0 263 19752 5
Sold and Seduced *Michelle Styles*	978 0 263 19753 2

MEDICAL ROMANCE™

His Very Own Wife and Child *Caroline Anderson*	
	978 0 263 19788 4
The Consultant's New-Found Family *Kate Hardy*	
	978 0 263 19789 1
A Child to Care For *Dianne Drake*	978 0 263 19790 7
His Pregnant Nurse *Laura Iding*	978 0 263 19791 4

MILLS & BOON®

0107 Gen Std LP

Live the emotion

FEBRUARY 2007 LARGE PRINT TITLES

ROMANCE™

Purchased by the Billionaire *Helen Bianchin*	978 0 263 19423 4
Master of Pleasure *Penny Jordan*	978 0 263 19424 1
The Sultan's Virgin Bride *Sarah Morgan*	978 0 263 19425 8
Wanted: Mistress and Mother *Carol Marinelli*	978 0 263 19426 5
Promise of a Family *Jessica Steele*	978 0 263 19427 2
Wanted: Outback Wife *Ally Blake*	978 0 263 19428 9
Business Arrangement Bride *Jessica Hart*	978 0 263 19429 6
Long-Lost Father *Melissa James*	978 0 263 19430 2

HISTORICAL ROMANCE™

Mistaken Mistress *Margaret McPhee*	978 0 263 19382 4
The Inconvenient Duchess *Christine Merrill*	978 0 263 19383 1
Falcon's Desire *Denise Lynn*	978 0 263 19384 8

MEDICAL ROMANCE™

The Sicilian Doctor's Proposal *Sarah Morgan*	978 0 263 19335 0
The Firefighter's Fiancé *Kate Hardy*	978 0 263 19336 7
Emergency Baby *Alison Roberts*	978 0 263 19337 4
In His Special Care *Lucy Clark*	978 0 263 19338 1
Bride at Bay Hospital *Meredith Webber*	978 0 263 19533 0
The Flight Doctor's Engagement *Laura Iding*	978 0 263 19534 7